THE SPINELESS PORCUPINE

"This whimsical allegory about diversity and inclusion is emotionally honest in a way that sticks with you. It carries such hard-hitting insights on what builds (or destroys) a sensation of trust and belonging in a community. Definitely the perfect book for restoring a sense of self-worth in someone who feels like they've never fit in. And for those doing the hard work of replacing suspicion and bias with teamwork and reconciliation, it provides much-needed lessons of compassion toward self and others."

—Carin Taylor,
Chief Diversity Officer at Workday

"This story of a porcupine without quills fighting for respect and recognition in a sharp, prickly, and antagonistic world is so poignant and relatable. As the little porcupine discovers her true values and stops being so motivated by the priorities of others, the reader is invited to do the same. This book reminds you that even when the world demands cruelty and competition, you can still choose love, joy, cooperation, and creativity. It's a gentle lesson, but an unforgettable one."

—Vivian Wong,
Group Vice President at Oracle & Board Director

"In a world of silencings, what we need are stories spoken aloud. And SAY has done just this. Addressing LGBTQ+ visibility and people on the edge, they have amplified stories for people who have felt on the edge of faith, on the edge of power, and on the edge of themselves. This is a book to soothe the heart, and to deepen courage, and to expand the imagination."

—Pádraig Ó Tuama,
Poet & Theologian

"As a former preacher and Christian speaker, I love great allegories because they can be 'sticky' ways to teach crucial lessons. In creating *The Spineless Porcupine*, SAY has given all of us who've ever submitted to the immense pressure to conform to rigid norms or incongruent expectations the realization that we need to grow a "spine" even if we, like Mattie, were born spineless. (I also love a good play on words!)

"However, it's rare that we can generate this kind of courage on our own. Like Mattie, most of us need unconditionally loving guides, like Pearson, who've already experienced this great self-awakening. They will help us see not only that we are not alone, but that who we truly are is what the best parts of the world are waiting for us to contribute. This book aptly captures my decades-long journey from looking to the American Evangelical 'circus' to give me my tenuous worth, to believing today that all of our worth is sourced in the One who made us who we are and who loves us without reservations."

—Rev. Dr. Ken Fong,
Retired Pastor & Asian America Podcast Host

FOREWORD BY PAUL YOUNG, AUTHOR OF **THE SHACK**

THE
SPINELESS
PORCUPINE

Why Our Differences Are Superpowers

SAY YANG

ILLUMIFY
MEDIA.COM
WE BRING YOUR BOOK TO LIFE!

Published by
Illumify Media Global
www.IllumifyMedia.com
"We bring your book to life!"

Library of Congress Control Number: 2020923077

Paperback ISBN: 978-1-947360-19-8
eBook ISBN: 978-1-947360-18-1

Typeset by Jennifer Clark
Cover design by Debbie Lewis

Printed in the United States of America

Dedicated to the spineless porcupine in all of us

CONTENTS

SAY WHAT?

You might be wondering, *why is your first name in all caps?* And, *how do I pronounce SAY?* It is indeed pronounced as it's written, as in "*say* something." Here's the story behind my name:

SAY has been my nickname since 2009. They are the initials for my full name, Sarah Allis Yang (which is why it's all capital letters). It's also reflective of my nature of always having something to SAY, and hopefully helpful insights at that.

Allis is my birth name. Like Mattie, the spineless porcupine you are about to meet, I was given a different name when I learned how to perform. I was renamed Sarah in the circus of evangelical ministry. For Mattie, she was renamed Juniper as she performed headliner tricks under the legendary big top of Circus Planet. I wanted to include both Allis and Sarah in my new name because my time as both made me who I am today. I also wanted to define myself on my own terms and not on those of others.

The final reason I chose SAY is because it's a non-binary name in terms of gender, which fits me better. I've lived 20 years as male presenting and 18 years as female presenting. I'm also an Asian American Queer Christian. Like Mattie, I never fit into neat binary categories and I'm continually building bridges between seemingly opposing groups. Both "she/her" and "he/him" pronouns don't fit me. What does fit me is "they/them."

I love that my pronouns are both singular and plural because it reminds me every time I hear it that I am never alone. The Divine is with me wherever I go, whoever I'm with, whatever I do. I appreciate the constant reminder.

And, just like Mattie and Pearson, I now find myself in the wilderness, rediscovering who I truly am and finding community there. I hope you'll join me on the journey of reclaiming our true selves. The best gift we can give this world is to unapologetically be ourselves and to inhabit the fullness of who we are. See you in the wilderness ...

"You give to the world your greatest gift
when you're being yourself."
- *Deepak Chopra*

FOREWORD

We all love a good story. Whether around a campfire or before bedtime or with a group of friends or strangers, Story has a way of capturing and transporting us to places we may have never imagined but can deeply feel.

As a boy, one of my greatest experiences was sitting with the elders, the older folk, and listening to them spin the Stories of their history, of mishaps and victories, of loves lost and found. I am now becoming one of those older ones and nothing much has changed. Today, I still see a waiting presence in the eyes of the younger ones, and wrapped inside their questions is the longing to be invited and Inside.

Story is not only verbal but visual. If we don't see it on a screen, we can watch it unfold in our imaginations, the cadence of words with their sounds crafting a tapestry in which we find ourselves, and then these becoming little treasures that we too can pass along. And while a Story might not be real, it is True.

Why our resonance with Story? One reason for this is because we *are* each a Story. Every human being is a Story. The younger ones are an unfolding Story while an elderly person is a treasure house in which Story sits and waits to be heard. You can see Story in the hands, and in the lines on the faces and the wrinkles that guard the smiles. A good Story always has multifaceted texture.

Another reason is that Story has the power to slip Truth past our 'Watchful Dragons,' as C.S. Lewis would say. We all have our Watchful Dragons, children the least unless they have been hurt. Dragons have been trained to guard the inner person, and they are usually stationed in the mind, armed with scales and talons of logic and training, watching to make sure nothing untoward gets too deep within the softness of our emotions and hope. Dragons don't believe such things exist—hope, courage, authentic kindness, wonder, and even love. Dragons watch over our stories because they are afraid that should we find our voices, we may indeed discover that all we secretly hoped for might not be true or real. Or perhaps, they are afraid they might be after all.

Dragons aren't truly evil. They are there to protect us, and sadly, some of us do need protecting, at least for a while. And then someone tells a Story, a Story that builds a bigger Inside than an Outside—with doors. And these doors have no locks; they are simply invitations. And one suddenly finds oneself Inside, and even for the briefest of moments, we hear something for ourselves, a Whisper that says, "You belong here." If we trust the Storyteller, we stay longer and listen a little more closely. And if we let it, wonder and other mysterious forces will actually, for a time, drown out the Dragon's voices. Sometimes even Dragons listen. Eventually, we'll leave the Outside and the Dragons will begin to shout again. But though they may speak loudly, they cannot drown out the whispers. And from such Whispers grow beautiful and wondrous things like a Tree of Life.

Many Adults and Dragons have made pacts; they have promised to defend and protect each other. Some Adults don't remember living without Dragons, and so they depend

on them. But Children, still innocent, have no Dragons—
they only have Whispers. And let me tell you a secret: Adults
with Dragons are still Children who simply can't hear as well
because of noisy Dragons. So, what should we do? We tell
Story! And Story will begin to heal the broken places where
Dragons have caused their damage. And with such Story
grow the Whispers. Here is the most amazing thing: Dragons, too, can be healed.

Listen, you can hear the Whispers too.

"You belong here!"

"You are not alone."

"You are not the stranger you thought you were."

"It is safe to be yourself."

"You matter."

"You are a Story, uniquely one-of-a-kind, precious, and
important for everyone to hear."

"Everyone you meet is a Story too. All you have to do is
ask."

In your hands is a Story. It is a Good Story and a True
Story. As you read it or listen to it, tell the Dragons in your
inside world to calm down for a while, to sit and listen, too.
And just perhaps, you and your Dragons are in for a
wonderful and healing adventure.

—William Paul Young, author of *The Shack, Cross Roads, Eve*

PART I:

THE CLAN

1

WHAT IS A PORCUPINE
WITHOUT SPINES?

IN A DENSE FOREST, DURING A BRUTAL WISCONSIN winter storm, Josephine gave birth. The tiny newborn had the cutest face, so tender and captivating. Almost immediately after she came out of the womb, her big, sparkling eyes locked with her mother for what seemed to be an eternity. And Josephine knew, as she gazed into her newborn's eyes, that she was exactly the commander the insular clan needed to bring about a new era. But there was one major difference with this porcupine from every other born before or after her—she was born without spines. Unlike other porcupettes, whose soft spines start to harden into quills within a few hours of their birth, this porcupette had no spines at all.

Spencer, her father and the commander of the elite porcupine clan, was devastated. Porcupines pride themselves on their unique natural defenses—even going as far as to consider themselves a superior species, only affiliating with other porcupines. As the mighty commander responsible for leading and protecting the clan, his quills were his sense of identity and worth.

He and Josephine had two other porcupettes—Trevor and Jasmine, though they didn't seem to have the heart and character required to succeed Spencer as commander. So he and Josephine decided to have one more porcupette. Both had a hopeful inkling that their youngest would be the commander who would usher in a greater era for their clan.

But, looking at the newborn, he saw just a tiny, frail, worthless animal before him and felt humiliated to call her one of his own. Spencer screamed at his partner while she was recovering from the difficult birth, "I don't know what she is, but she is not mine. We are a fearsome species, not to be trifled with. But she, or whatever it is ... is not of our kind. After all, what is a porcupine without spines?"

He openly accused Josephine of having an affair and kicked her and the newborn out of their den. He would not give the baby a name or even acknowledge her. He commanded Trevor, the firstborn (who he had now designated to succeed him as commander) and Jasmine, his eldest daughter, to renounce all ties to their mother and newborn sister. He told them that their mother had brought shame upon the family for giving birth to the world's first spineless porcupine-like creature. "There's no way she'll live for very long without a coat of dark spines to shield her delicate, anemic skin. She'll never survive in the cruel, harsh Northeast conditions," Spencer said. The truth was that, though he was tough on the outside, he was scared to death on the inside that he would get hurt and be humiliated. Porcupines obsess with protecting themselves from pain, both outside and in. And he didn't want to risk getting attached to a porcupette that he might lose soon or that might suggest that he was weak.

So, Josephine and her infant went from the center of the clan to being exiled to the freezing outskirts of the porcupine community, at the base of the foreboding, saw-toothed hills. Afraid she might injure her defenseless baby with her quills when she nursed her, Josephine stood like a statue with her underbelly jutted forward to avoid accidentally poking her. As her baby girl struggled to take sips, she focused on transmitting all her love and strength to the little one through her gaze. Josephine wanted more than anything to cuddle her in her arms but instead was forced to communicate her love through her eyes and voice. While staring into her baby's eyes, she would whisper over and over, "I believe in you. I love you, sweetie. I know one day you'll grow up and become a mighty warrior just like your father."

Indeed, the little spineless one did have a fighting spirit. Against all odds, she pulled her way through the critical first six months of life. Her mom decided to name her Madeline or Mattie for short, which means "Strength in Battle, Strong in War."

2

WELCOME TO THE PRICKLE

SOON AFTER MATTIE LEARNED TO TALK, SHE SPENT many nights asking her mom questions like, "What am I? Where do porcupines come from? What's a clan? Where is our clan?"

Josephine retold the fabled history of porcupines being one of the most evolved creatures because of their natural defenses. While they were feared and respected by most animals, porcupines were known for sticking to their own kind and avoiding other animals. Therefore, anything or anyone that was different was immediately shunned.

Mattie's paternal great-great-grandfather, Chris, was a very proud, wise, and charismatic leader. He had convinced several prickles of ten or twelve porcupines to band together to form the first porcupine clan so they could claim the lushest part of the forest from occupation by their predators. Chris created the first-ever warrior school to train all porcupines to identify their enemies and other animals. They also learned how to work together to take down mountain lions, coyotes, fishers, and bobcats. After months of training, they engaged in a great battle and caught their predators off guard. United as one under Chris' strategy, they overcame them, claimed the best part of the forest, and had kept it ever since. Soon after this, Chris was appointed as commander. Since then, a descendant from his lineage had carried the responsibility of leading and protecting the clan alongside a clan council elected by the other porcupines.

"I'm a descendant of the mighty commander," Mattie said, her eyes widening.

"Yes, my love," Josephine answered.

Mattie stood up and inquired, "And we're part of the first-ever porcupine clan occupying the best part of the forest?"

Josephine shrugged her shoulders, not knowing how to explain that they've been exiled. Mattie was too excited to notice her mom's hesitation. Instead, she jumped up and down and exclaimed as she shot her paw into the air, "I'm going to make my clan proud and live up to the great lineage of commanders!"

Josephine smiled with a tinge of sadness, knowing it would be an uphill battle for Mattie to be accepted, let alone make the clan proud. But it was difficult to stop Mattie once she had made up her mind about something. She was very clever, persistent, and curious.

One night, when Josephine saw a bobcat hunting for porcupines in the clan, she insisted that Mattie hide with her in a nearby cave in the saw-toothed hills for a few days. Instead, Mattie waited until her mom fell asleep, sharpened a branch into a makeshift knife, carried it in her mouth, and snuck out of the cave into the dead of night several evenings in a row looking for the bobcat. Thankfully, Josephine caught on to Mattie's midnight escapades when her daughter forgot to cover the cave entrance after a long, exhausting search for the bobcat. This confirmed to Josephine that Mattie had her great, great grandfather's tenacity and craftiness to be a trail-blazer. She knew she had to reason with her stubborn daughter and explain exactly why she couldn't go on these hunting adventures.

"I don't know what to do with you, my love," sighed Josephine.

"What do you mean?" Mattie pondered.

"You have the heart of a commander, yet you are so vulnerable."

"How so?"

"You see these spiky things on me?"

Mattie nodded. "Mine will grow in soon, right?"

Misty-eyed, Josephine was moved by Mattie's hopeful innocence and whispered, "No, sweetie."

"Am I the only one like me?" the naked porcupine asked, as she trembled awaiting her mother's response.

Slowly Josephine nodded her head, looking into her daughter's eyes compassionately. Mattie's heart sunk to the ground as she speculated, "Is that why we're out here and the rest of the porcupines are over there?"

Josephine nodded again, and this time a tear escaped her eye. Being spineless, Mattie had heightened intuition and could sense how heartbroken her mom was to be away from the rest of their family and clan.

"That's OK, Mommy. I'll get us back in. It's not your fault I was born this way. I'll prove to all of them that what makes me different is my superpower and when they realize that, they will welcome us back with open arms."

Josephine shook her head and chuckled at her preco-cious porcupette's naivete, "Porcupines don't like different, my dear."

"They will after they meet me. You said that I have the heart of a commander, right?"

Josephine hesitated. It seemed like an impossible road for Mattie to become the clan's leader. But she also couldn't bring herself to lie, so she gave a knowing smile. "Baby, you have more courage and ingenuity than any porcupine I know. You are the first of your kind and the first to the fight."

That's all the encouragement Mattie needed as she said, "Then different is exactly what their next commander will be!"

3

THE CLAN COUNCIL

ONE HOT SUMMER AFTERNOON, WHILE YOUNG MATTIE helped her mom gather twigs on top of a pine tree, she saw a crowd of eight porcupines heading their way.

"Mommy, look!" Mattie shouted. Her heart leaped at the sight of other porcupines.

Josephine squinted and put her paw above her eyes to see into the horizon. "Ah, yes. The annual warrior school final."

"I wanna go, I wanna go!" Mattie pleaded.

"Are you sure, baby girl? You could get hurt in training." Josephine's face was full of concern at the thought of Mattie being around other porcupines.

"Mommy, please! I can do it. I'll prove it to you," begged Mattie.

Josephine looked into Mattie's glimmering eyes, full of excitement as she vigilantly watched the porcupines take the final. Josephine relented, "If you are sure you want this, I can talk to the clan council—but no promises."

"Yippie! Yes, please do. Tell them that I want to help protect our clan and make our commander proud. Maybe then, they'll take us back!" Mattie shouted.

Josephine shook her head. Mattie wanted what all kids want, to belong and make the family proud. She knew that Mattie wouldn't stop asking her about it unless she at least tried.

Josephine came up with a plan. She had known the governor of the clan council, Ethan, since she was little. Ethan, Josephine, and Spencer went to warrior school together, and although Ethan had also tried to win Josephine's heart to become his partner, Spencer's once kind and tender heart triumphed in the end. Even so, Ethan had always treated her with respect and graciousness.

She knew Ethan wouldn't allow anything bad to happen to her even if she disobeyed Spencer's banishment and returned to plead her case for Mattie to attend warrior school. The next evening, Josephine went to the clan council, where Ethan was presiding with Spencer by his side. When a couple of young warrior porcupines tried to stop her from approaching, Ethan waved them down saying, "Let her in."

It was the first time she had seen both the governor and Spencer since he had forced her out of their home. She began, "No porcupine has ever been banned from warrior school."

"But she's not a porcupine. She has no quills!" Spencer quipped.

Josephine's eyes darted toward her estranged partner. "She's a fighter just like her father."

Spencer resented the association to Mattie, "She's not mine!"

Ethan interrupted, "Enough, you two. The real question here is, how can Mattie be a warrior if she can't even defend herself?"

"Well, we won't know unless we give her a chance," Josephine said.

"She's not of our species. Plus, all the others would have

to avoid her so she wouldn't get hurt. We would be doing this for her benefit, not ours," Spencer said, feigning compassion.

Josephine was used to Spencer manipulating others to get his way. She knew she had to act fast. "How about if she stays in a back corner away from the other porcupines?" she said.

"And wears a bell around her neck to let the others know when she's close by so they can avoid her?" Spencer said.

The council looked at each other and nodded their heads. As much as Josephine wanted to protect Mattie from feeling even more different than she already did, she knew that this would be the only way for her precious daughter to get her wish. She reluctantly agreed to their terms.

4

DING, DING, DING

DING, DING, DING, RANG THE BELL AROUND MATTIE'S neck as she gingerly made a beeline to the back corner. She tried her best not to stand out. But what could Mattie do? Not only did her bell chime annoyingly every time she moved a millimeter, but she was also the only hairless one among a sea of dark, spiny-coated critters.

She desperately wanted to connect with the other six porcupines in her class, especially her older brother and sister, who she had often heard about from her mom but had never met. Little did she know that Trevor and Jasmine had spent several nights plotting with their father on how to stop Mattie from ever returning to the clan.

As each male porcupine walked in, Mattie said excitedly, "Hi, are you Trevor?" And to each female porcupine, she asked, "Hello, are you Jasmine?" When Trevor and Jasmine finally walked in, Mattie smiled with a glimmer in her eye. She saw the resemblance and couldn't help but move toward them. Ding, ding, ding.

"Hello! Are you Trevor and Jasmine?" she asked shyly.

Trevor laughed viciously. "Yeah. And you must be, 'Freak of Nature.' I heard so much about you!"

Jasmine looked Mattie up and down with disdain. "What in the heavens are you? You're on the wrong planet."

Trevor motioned for the class to gather around Mattie. "I have a riddle for everyone. What's a porcupine with no spines?"

Jasmine responded on cue, "Dead meat."

Trevor hobbled mockingly around the class yelling, "Look, I'm Mattie. I'm a free meal on wheels."

Boisterous laughter filled the classroom followed by, ding, ding, ding, as Mattie made her way away from the prickle of porcupines, weeping. Before she was able to get far though, Trevor shoved Jasmine into Mattie, piercing her with hundreds of razor-sharp quills.

"Well, look at that. She finally has quills," said Trevor.

Jasmine whispered venomously to Mattie as they were face to face, "This is for taking mom away from us."

5

STRENGTH IN BATTLE,
STRONG IN WAR

MATTIE HOBBLED IN PAIN ALL THE WAY BACK TO THEIR den on the outskirts of the village. Her mom was already watching the horizon expectantly waiting for Mattie's return. The glee of seeing Mattie quickly shifted to horror when Josephine saw Mattie hobbling and bleeding. She ran toward Mattie with tears streaming down her face.

After years of practice, Josephine stopped at the exact distance from her daughter to avoid piercing her with her own quills. But that day of all days, she would have given anything to be closer. Mattie wanted to collapse into a ball on the floor, but the spines stuck in her skin prevented her from doing so. She remained standing, though her heart was in the dirt.

Through her tears, Mattie said, "Mommy, am I a freak of nature? Did I come from another planet?"

"What in the world are you talking about?" Josephine replied, feeling a sharp pang in her heart.

Mattie, unable to hear a word through the pain, "Do you wish you never had me? Then you'd still be with Dad, Jasmine, and Trevor." Mattie wept.

Josephine saw the anguish on her precious daughter's

face and knew it was finally time for her to do what she'd wanted to do ever since Mattie was born. Josephine pressed all of her quills into a nearby tree to remove them. This would mean they would be defenseless for at least two months. She approached Mattie and gently removed the bell from her neck. She caressed Mattie's face, and looking deeply into her eyes, said, "There's not a day that goes by where I don't thank the heavens for giving me someone as phenomenal as you."

Exhausted, Mattie fell asleep as Josephine whispered into her ear, "Everything's going to be OK."

As the sun rose, Josephine carefully removed the last of the spines that Mattie was so cruelly punctured with. As the last one was removed from her, Mattie mumbled, "Well, now I know what it feels like to have quills. We've traded places."

Tears fell from Josephine's eyes as she wondered how Mattie could have such a good-humored attitude about the horrors that had happened to her. She was revealing that she had the heart and character of a warrior.

Josephine carried Mattie, still sleeping, to a crook high in a nearby tree and made a makeshift den. Nearby some bats hovered. They seemed to sense their vulnerability. Frightened, Josephine cradled Mattie close to her, but thankfully, the bats did not attack. They seemed almost protective of the two defenseless porcupines.

When Mattie finally awoke the next evening, her mom glanced over and smiled. She placed some fresh bark in front of her daughter to eat. For the very first time, Josephine held Mattie close to her. Like going from hell to heaven in a moment, her sensitive skin went from aching from the hundreds of wounds to the soothing bliss of being nestled in her mom's arms.

After a long time gazing into her daughter's eyes, Josephine said, "Did I ever tell you why I named you Madeline?"

"Why, Mama?" Mattie asked, resting her head against her mom's chest to listen to her heartbeat for the first time.

"When I first looked into your eyes, I saw your father. You know, he wasn't always so mean."

"What happened?" Mattie asked.

"His father, Steven, was killed by coyotes soon after Trevor was born. Your grandfather was a warm, compassionate, loving porcupine and wanted to form alliances with the other forest animals. You're a lot like him," Josephine said. "Your father resented losing him so soon. He perceived his father's kindness as weakness, unbecoming a porcupine. From that day forward, he vowed to protect the community at all costs. In his mind, this meant being nothing like his father."

Josephine caressed Mattie's face and looked into her eyes, reminiscing on her determination to hunt the bobcat as a young porcupette. "But when I first met your father, he was a true warrior—one who was motivated by courage and love, not fear and rage. You have the heart of a fighter, Mattie. That's why I named you Madeline, which means 'Strength in battle, strong in war.'" It was true. Mattie could not stay away from a battle for long.

Soon after Mattie recovered from her wounds, she tied the bell back around her neck. She practiced moving as quietly as she could. Out of her desperation to be accepted, she also began eating fewer twigs so that there would be less of her to avoid. However, Mattie knew her body would not be the only key to her success. She would also have to rely on her mind.

Spring came and the warrior school final, held on each summer solstice, was quickly approaching. In the final, a student must prove they could defend themselves against a dreaded coyote attack. Coyotes were one of the few predators that knew the prickly creatures' vulnerability: their bare bellies. The teachers would stage a surprise attack and pounce like a coyote. The young porcupine would either have to figure out a way to escape or stay belly down and quickly turn its back on the predator, activating their quills and lashing them with their tail. Most of warrior school centered around mastering this tricky three-step maneuver, also known as the DAB move:

Drop to the ground,
Activate the quills,
Break out the tail.

Mattie knew that, unlike the other porcupines, her entire body was vulnerable. Plus, she was not a fast runner because of her short legs. She spent many sleepless nights mulling over how she could pass the final and prove to the entire community that she was a warrior like her father.

While staring up at the stars one night, nibbling on a twig, she saw a faint web in the moonlight nearby. A famished spider was feasting on a poor fly caught in his trap. Mattie inquired of the little spider, "Wow, you're a hungry little fella, aren't you?"

The spider said, "Yeah. What's it to ya, toots?" He continued eating.

Mattie replied, "Sorry, didn't mean to be rude. By the way, nice web. What's your name?"

"Mikey, what's yours?"

"Mattie, the spineless porcupine."

He chuckled. "I knew the second part. Well, you're the first porcupine that's ever bothered talking to me."

"Yeah, that's because we tend to stick to our own kind,"

Mattie muttered with her head hanging low in embarrassment.

As he continued feasting, Mikey said, "That's a shame 'cos you can learn a lot from other creatures."

"Like what?" Mattie asked, envying Mikey's hearty meal. She regretted cutting down on her twig intake.

"Well, do you know how to weave a web?" Mikey asked.

Suddenly excited, Mattie tossed the twig over her shoulder and shouted, "That's brilliant! Would you teach me how to build traps?"

Mikey nodded. "If you'll carry me around on your back so I can explore more of the forest."

"Deal!" Mattie exclaimed.

6

THE WARRIOR SCHOOL FINALS

IT WAS THE LONGEST DAY OF THE YEAR, WHICH MEANT it was time for the warrior school finals. Since the humiliating incident with her older brother and sister about a year ago, Mattie had not visited the clan. If it were not for her spineless skin and the bell around her neck, the others would not have recognized her. She walked into the warrior school with her head held high, Mikey hiding in a crevice of her ear—for moral support—and a forced smile on her face. Mattie refused to allow them to see how scared she was. Inside, she kept repeating the meaning of her name, "Strength in battle. Strong in war." Mikey sensed her fear and encouraged her by saying, "You got this. You're awesome."

Hearing Mikey's pep talk eased her tension. Trevor's jaw dropped when he heard Mattie approaching. Quickly he tapped Jasmine on the shoulder. She was in mid-conversation with her female clique about which porcupine was the hottest warrior. Trevor gasped and said, "Jasmine, what is *she* doing here?"

Mattie headed to the back corner and did her best to ignore the uproar caused by her arrival. Walter, one of the teachers, asked everyone to calm down. He said to Mattie, "You do know it's finals day, right?"

"That's why I'm here," Mattie said as she nodded.

With a concerned look, Walter said, "Are you sure you want to do this? We're not going to take it easy on you because you're spineless."

Mattie smiled. "If anything, please be tougher on me. That'll help me."

Walter walked away puzzled. "OK, enough with the ruckus. Mattie's here to take the final."

Jasmine quipped, "I guess she didn't get enough quills from her last visit."

The class erupted in laughter. Mikey glared at Jasmine from within Mattie's ear. He shot a web at her face quickly before disappearing back into a crevice.

"What the hell?" Jasmine screamed and flailed as she swatted the freshly dispensed mesh off her face.

Mattie giggled softly, which helped relieve her stress. She put her paw near her ear so Mikey could tap it, as they were accustomed to doing to celebrate wins.

Walter yelled, "Enough, all of you! This isn't playtime. Stay focused! Have you forgotten about your finals? Let's go!"

The class entered the heavily brushed forest on the outskirts, near Mattie's and Josephine's home. After exploring the entire backwoods several times with Mikey, she knew these trees like the back of her paw. He had also coached her on exactly where to place all her booby traps.

Walter gathered the prickle around him. "OK, everyone. We'll have each of you go into the forest one at a time. We can attack you at any moment, and you must respond within three seconds, proving that you have mastered the

Coyote Tactic." Walter looked directly at Mattie and continued, "Or escape somehow. If you don't, it's another year of
warrior school. Got it?"

"Yes, sir!" the prickle shouted in unison, except for
Mattie who never learned that protocol.

"Who's the brave one that wants to go first?" Walter
asked.

Trevor shot up his paw and shouted militantly, "Me,
sir!"

And with that, each porcupine lined up behind Trevor.
Mattie went to the very back of the line simply to avoid
getting pricked by the others.

To no one's surprise, Trevor passed in a record one and a
half seconds upon being attacked. He immediately planted
himself belly down, aimed his quills precisely at his assailant,
and thrashed his tail wildly. Jasmine was in second place
with a time of two seconds, accurately targeting her
hundreds of tiny, barbed needles at her mock attacker while
protecting her soft belly.

As each porcupine took their turn through the dense
forest, Mattie diligently observed and studied where the
teachers often attacked. Most of the porcupines failed,
primarily because they were disoriented in unfamiliar terri-
tory. The teachers strategically hid themselves in what looked
like safe, open spaces only to surprise the unsuspecting
young warriors from behind. By the time they realized they
were being attacked, it was too late to engage the three-step
DAB move to drop, activate, and break out their tail. Others
froze in fear instead of trying to escape.

When it was finally Mattie's turn, all the porcupines
gathered around to watch. Jasmine tried to intimidate
Mattie. "It's not too late to give up, you know?"

Mikey peered out and shot another web at Jasmine's
face.

"OMG, there are spider webs everywhere in this dump

of a place!" Jasmine shouted as she flung her limbs wildly to get the strands off herself.

The class looked at each other perplexed because she seemed to be the only one encountering these mysterious webs. Mattie smirked but kept her eyes fixed on the forest in front of her, unhooked the bell around her neck, and shuffled in.

Her soft, bare skin shimmered in the fading sunlight as ominous bats emerged from their caves and circled above her. She was quivering and had no quills like the others to hide her fear—bats freaked her out. A late afternoon breeze passed through the foliage and rustled a few leaves nearby. Startled, Mattie shivered, then squeaked loudly. It was an involuntary reflex when she was terrified. The class giggled.

Mikey whispered into her ear, "It's OK, I'm here. I got you."

Suddenly, Walter leaped toward them. Mattie dodged him and ran with all the speed her stumpy legs could provide. She turned the corner while Mikey peeked out of her ear to see precisely how far the mock assailant was trailing behind them. That's when the trusty spider whispered into Mattie's ear, "Now."

Mattie whacked the trigger branch they had set together a few days earlier. As Walter followed them around the corner, a net on the ground snapped shut behind him and swept him four feet up in the air. Dangling high above the shocked class, Walter grabbed the net for balance and shouted at Mattie, "What is this? Get me down now!"

Gasping for air, Mattie turned around, smiled, and quipped, "Only if I pass."

7

MS. POPULARITY

FOLLOWING HER TRIUMPH AT THE FINAL, ALL THE porcupines, other than Mattie's estranged family, wanted to be her friend. She became very good at anticipating what each porcupine liked: undivided attention, a good joke, berries, matchmaking, gossip, or intellectual banter. Her lonely upbringing, with only her mom and Mikey's company out in the wilderness, caused her to be hyper-aware and tuned into other creatures' preferences. This was all to help her avoid the rejection which had caused her so much pain growing up.

Mattie adapted well and grew in favor with the community to the point that she almost forgot she had no quills. She felt protected and clothed in the approval of her peers. Her bell went from being a source of shame to an adornment she was proud of. When others heard her coming, they would say, "Mattie's here!" Some porcupines even asked if they could put her bell around their own neck to try it out. Jasmine and her clique began to pay her attention as well. In her newfound fame, however, she spent less and less time with her mom and Mikey—those who had supported her when no one else would.

"We have to put a stop to this! She's making a fool of us," exclaimed Spencer to his children.

Trevor said, "But how? Everyone adores her. Ethan just commissioned her to build traps all around the community to keep predators away."

Spencer paced back and forth anxiously. He abruptly stopped and turned toward Trevor. "That's it! If we can prove that the traps are dangerous to the clan, they will turn against her."

It was a cold, winter night and Mattie was hard at work, with Mikey resting in her ear surveying the perimeter for potential trap locations. While they were coming down from a tree, something suddenly approached her out of the shadows. Mattie squeaked in fear involuntarily. It was Jasmine.

"Hey, Mattie," Jasmine said, not noticing Mikey who quickly hid in a crevice of her ear so as not to be seen.

Mattie sighed as she covered her ear, "Whew, I thought you were a coyote."

Jasmine said, "Nope, just one of your own. You know, I've been doing some thinking."

Mattie looked into Jasmine's eyes and for the first time, she did not see rage or fear. She could see their resemblance. Jasmine hastily looked to the ground.

"Anyhow, I just wanted you to know I really messed up. You're my little sister. I should be protecting you, not treating you so badly. I was just so jealous because I thought Mom loved you more than us," Jasmine confessed as tears welled up in her eyes.

Mattie's heart filled with empathy, knowing exactly what it was like to feel unwanted. She said, "No, that's not true. There's not a day that goes by when Mom doesn't want to be with you. She talks about all of you constantly. I know she misses you."

Jasmine looked up at Mattie with a faint smile, "Really?"

Mattie nodded and smiled.

"Well, I hope we can put the past behind us. Friends?" Jasmine proclaimed as she put her prickly paw out.

Jasmine then chuckled, "Sorry, force of habit."

Mattie shook it anyway. A few quills pierced her naked paw but inside, her heart leaped at finally reconciling with her estranged sister. Now, if she could only win over her father and brother, maybe they could all be reunited. Her heart swelled with hope as she imagined returning as a heroine to her clan.

As Jasmine headed off, Mattie uncovered her ear and Mikey peeked out. He said, "I have a bad feeling about her."

"What do you mean? She's my sister. Do you know how long I've been waiting for this?" Mattie asked him.

"She's up to something," Mikey said.

Mattie snapped back, "You're just jealous that I have other friends now."

"Wow, this has all really gotten to your head," Mikey said as he crawled off her. As he began to move away, Mikey said, "Well, now that you've got what you wanted, you won't be needing me anymore."

"Whatever, you're being totally irrational. Now I know why creatures stick to their own kind. You totally don't get me," Mattie snarled.

Mikey scampered into the forest, "I understand you perfectly, Mattie. But the most important question is, do you understand yourself?"

His words cut her to the core, but she quickly protested, "It's not like that. I want you in my life along with the porcupines."

"No, you don't, Mattie. All you care about is their

approval. And now you have it, congratulations." Mikey said as he scurried away.

She chased after him, but he quickly disappeared into the foliage covering the forest floor.

Mattie yelled, "Mikey, come back. I'm sorry."

But he didn't respond.

A few hours after Mikey had disappeared, she consoled herself by rationalizing that she finally did have everything she wanted—respect and acceptance of her clan, and most of all, her estranged family coming back into her life. Trading the friendship with one little spider for that of many with her own kind, she'd take that exchange. In her newfound fame, however, she grieved the loss of the only friend who had loved her when she had been a "nobody."

8

COUNTERBALANCE

Jasmine and Mattie were now almost as inseparable as their own shadows. Jasmine even came back with Mattie to her den in the outskirts of the forest. When Jasmine first arrived, Josephine touched her bare belly with Jasmine's, the porcupine equivalent of a long, deep embrace. They cried together for a long time.

Mattie showed Jasmine everything: how to navigate the dense forest, where to find shelter and food, and most importantly, how to build traps. They spent days working together to secure the forest's perimeter from predators.

One evening, Jasmine jumped up and down playfully as she stood in the net she had helped set up. Mattie was in a nearby tree tying a vine to the net below. "I don't get it. How do you stop it from trapping me?" asked Jasmine.

Mattie explained as she finished tying the knot, "Easy. Coyotes, bears, wolves, and fishers all weigh more than us." Mattie reached over and pointed to a large rock tied to the vine, "See this? It's a counterbalance for the snare. Only creatures heavier than this rock will get trapped."

"What about poor Walter then?" Jasmine asked.

Mattie climbed back down from the tree. "Oh, that was

a different kind of trap—a trigger trap. Those won't work for the perimeter unless someone is operating them all the time. You hungry?"

"Absolutely," Jasmine answered.

"Great. I'm craving berries. And we're almost done. Two more traps to go!"

Meanwhile, in the clan council, Spencer presented his case against Mattie's traps:

"As commander, it is my responsibility to protect the community. We have never been attacked on my watch. So why on earth do we need traps now? What if one of my warriors is escaping a coyote and gets ensnared instead? He'll be a helpless, hanging meal."

Ethan calmly responded, "I understand your concern, Spencer. Mattie promised that the traps would not trap porcupines, only predators. Why don't you come to the demonstration in a few days and see for yourself?"

"And what if they do?" Spencer demanded.

"Then I will see to it myself that she removes all the traps," Ethan replied.

"I have your word?" asked Spencer.

Ethan nodded and the clan council adjourned.

9

IT'S A TRAP

A STORM WAS BREWING IN THE DISTANCE WHEN THE entire clan council arrived for the demonstration. Mattie anxiously paced back and forth as bats hovered above. Mattie thought, "Why do those freakish bats always show up when something big is about to happen? Is it an omen?" She tried to shoo them away, but they just hovered higher above her.

Jasmine had gone missing after they had finished setting up the final trap. Mattie wondered if Trevor or Spencer had something to do with it. Maybe they were upset that Jasmine was spending so much time with her. Her mind was racing when Ethan approached.

"You ready, Mattie? We should get to it before the storm rolls in."

Mattie nodded. She explained the trap system to the council and asked for a brave volunteer to come forward to run through the trap. Spencer raised his hand. Mattie smiled. This was her chance to finally prove herself to her dad.

Mattie pointed to the net. "OK, go ahead and run through it as if you were being chased by a coyote."

Spencer circled around the net suspiciously, ran several feet away from the crowd, and then made a beeline toward the net. Right as Spencer was about to pass through, a piercing sound echoed through the forest. SNAP! Spencer flew high up into the air and dangled above the horrified council. They gasped and panicked in fear.

"Help me! I think it broke my leg!" Spencer shouted.

Chaos ensued as the council fled in every direction. Mattie stood mortified as she stared at her injured father. Ethan turned toward her and yelled, "Get him down now!"

Mattie quickly cut the vine without thinking and her father slammed to the ground with a loud thump. Ethan ran over to Spencer, who was rolling and yelping in pain. Spencer screamed, "Get me out of this thing!"

Ethan and Mattie struggled to detangle Spencer from the mess just as it began raining. In the process, Mattie sustained hundreds of quill punctures, but she could not feel them or even the pouring rain. All Mattie felt was her flushed face as a blanket of shame covered her from head to toe. In the back of her mind, she wondered if Mikey had sabotaged the traps out of revenge for her betrayal.

10

BANISHED

The first family reunion since Mattie was born four years ago was sadly under horrible circumstances. The special clan council trial was about to begin, and it was packed. Still recovering from the quill wounds, Mattie stood as the defendant, with her mom by her side. Trevor and Jasmine carried the injured Spencer in on a piece of wood and laid him on the opposite side as the plaintiff. Mattie tried to get Jasmine's attention but to no avail. There were many familiar faces. But when she smiled faintly at anyone, they snickered and looked disgusted.

Ethan slammed down the gavel. "Please present your case, Spencer."

Spencer spoke faintly, "As commander, I have an obligation to protect this community, so I volunteered to test the trap. If anyone is to get hurt, it should be me and no one else."

He shifted his body weakly and continued, "Looking at my current state, I think it is clear that Mattie is a liability to us. Porcupines are defined by their ability to protect themselves. Mattie's only defense and value was with her traps.

Now that we have proven that they are ineffective and even harmful, I question her place in this community."

The bell around Mattie's neck tinkled as she looked to the ground in shame.

Spencer persisted, "Even her bell poses a threat to us. It could give away our position to the coyotes who have hyper-sensitive hearing."

"That was your idea, Spencer!" Josephine angrily countered.

Spencer replied, "I wanted to protect her from the other porcupines. It was the only way for her to interact with us. But is it worth accommodating Mattie at the risk of the entire clan?"

Ethan looked at Mattie and asked, "Do you have anything to say?"

Silently she stood before the council with tears in her eyes. But inside, a violent torrent of thoughts flooded her mind, *If I don't belong with my own kind, where is my home? Even my own mom with all her love can't get too close without putting me at risk. No matter what I do or where I go, I'm destined to be hurt or hurt others. I even betrayed my only true friend and mentor, Mikey. I deserve to be banished.*

More sternly this time, Ethan asked, "Mattie, do you have anything to say for yourself?"

Glancing at Ethan, Mattie shook her head.

"OK, then. The council will convene and present our decision in an hour," said Ethan.

But Mattie had already sentenced herself. She took the bell off her neck, set it down before the council, and left.

11

MAN'S LAND

IN THE DEAD OF WINTER, JOSEPHINE FOUND AN abandoned den at the outermost edge of the community. She thought that a change of environment might do them good. But no matter how many blackberries she brought back to Mattie, or how many times she said, "I love you," or "It's OK, sweetie," nothing was getting through. Whenever Josephine looked into Mattie's eyes, Mattie turned away. She was convinced that there was nothing of value in her for her mom or anyone else to see.

When spring came, Mattie's quill wounds had healed. But her heart had not. She went to destroy all the traps around the perimeter, as charged to by the council. As she approached the first trap, she discovered the rock placed there as a counterbalance was missing. Then another and another. Mattie slowly became aware of her sister's betrayal. Mikey couldn't have moved them. It must have been Jasmine who had removed all of them. Mikey was a true friend who had been trying to protect her, but she hadn't seen or heard from him since the argument, and thanks to her stubbornness, she didn't know if she ever would again.

Mattie now realized that it's not just words or flesh and blood that determines loyalty and sincerity, but heart and actions. Mikey had always looked out for her best interests, and from then on, she decided that she would do her best not to discriminate against other creatures based on their species. She missed Mikey so much and wondered if he was even still alive.

Death was on her mind because sadly, some squirrels and raccoons had become victims of the net traps that had been left without their counterbalancing weights. When she cut these nets down, their carcasses landed at her feet. She felt guilty and wished she were one of them. She succumbed to the ruminating trance of self-hatred that brewed inside of her. *It's all my fault. I always screw everything up. If I had heeded Mikey's warning, this never would've happened.*

The truth was that it was easier for Mattie to blame herself instead of Jasmine because this gave her a semblance of control. Though the unweighted traps were clearly Jasmine's fault, Mattie couldn't control Jasmine's actions, and accepting the fact that she couldn't stop tragedies from occurring was scarier to her than succumbing to a spiral of shame.

One evening, in the distance, she heard a coyote howl and went toward the sound. Before she knew it, she was running full force, seeking a quick end to what she judged her miserable, doomed life.

As she ran, the landscape changed, and fewer and fewer trees surrounded her. She scurried by areas of shrubs, grass, and gravel she had never seen before. The plants were well-manicured and in systematic patterns unlike the wild, native forest. Mattie finally stopped to gather her breath. It was in this stillness that she felt a strange, low vibration shaking the ground. It came in intervals and got stronger, accompanied by a zoom, then faded away.

Confused, she began to wonder if it was a coyote. After

all the horror stories she had heard about them, she had never encountered one in the flesh. And those who had rarely survived to tell the tale. A surge of panic filled her heart, and though she had initially wanted to die, her strong survival instinct and fear of pain took over. Mattie hobbled as quickly as she could to hide in a well-trimmed lime green shrub next to a black, shiny surface on the ground. Dry branches pricked her skin, triggering flashbacks of her sister's stabbing quills and her father struggling to free himself from the net. Her eyes welled with tears as the visceral reminders of her humiliation overwhelmed her.

The ground began shaking again as she looked up to see an enormous, shiny blue, rectangular beast with circular feet moving quickly toward her. It screeched to a halt right next to her, and she froze in utter terror. Mattie had never seen such a structured beast before in her native forest nor the creature that proceeded to emerge from its interior. Creak, slam, stomp, stomp, stomp.

Whatever the being was, it was headed straight for her.

The creature stood upright like the gigantic apes she learned about in warrior school. Mattie still paralyzed with fear, involuntarily trembled in the bright green bush. She did her best to hide her dark, defenseless body within the sparse shrubbery as the creature's shadow suddenly loomed over her. She looked up at the mammoth being standing on two legs towering above. Mattie shivered and couldn't help letting out a squeak. At that moment, she hated everything about herself. She remembered Trevor's voice, *You're a free meal on wheels.*

Giant hands enveloped Mattie, and no matter how hard she squirmed and twisted, she could not escape. The creature held Mattie up to its face, looked intently at her, and sniffed her. She thought, *I am truly "dead meat."* After carefully examining her entire body, the creature exclaimed, "Eureka!"

She was baffled with her ability to comprehend what it

shouted at the top of its lungs. Though she fought with all her might to break free, the creature carried her back to the shiny blue, rectangular-shaped beast. Then the creature seemed to open up the beast, which creaked in response. With horror, she saw that they were entering its gigantic mouth. Mattie wondered, *Did we just get swallowed?*

Mattie looked around for a way of escape through the mouth of this blue beast. But before she could free herself from its grip, the creature placed her within a confined space that resembled a small and rectangular cave. It was dark except where a little light shone through a couple of circular openings on each of the four sides of this wood-like object. Unfortunately, she could barely fit her paws, let alone her head through these openings. She felt relieved though that she could feel a slight breeze through them and she breathed deeply. She tried pushing the covering above her, each of the wooden sides surrounding her, and the floor beneath her, but nothing budged. She pondered, *What's with this creature that loves rectangular objects? How bizarre! Why can't they surround themselves with the wild, unpredictable shapes of the forest?* No matter how hard she tried, this rectangular wooden object kept her locked within it quite securely. She was caught, just like her dad and those animals had been in her traps. *How ironic, maybe I'm getting what I deserve.* Mattie resigned herself to whatever fate awaited her.

Then she heard the creak again and her surroundings rumbled with a loud noise, the same low vibration she had heard when she hid in the bush. Momentum threw her toward one of the walls of the wooden rectangular object as the vibrations became progressively louder.

She began freaking out and blaming herself for her predicament. Her thoughts were abruptly interrupted when a pulsing rhythm and melody increased in volume and resonated throughout the beast. That's when the ape-like creature began mimicking the music, banging along with the rhythm enthusiastically. Whoever these bizarre beings were, they were forcibly taking her away from her homeland into the great unknown.

PART II:

THE CIRCUS

12

THE BIG TOP

Mattie awoke to a Rhesus monkey poking her face. He had a round red headpiece with decorative yellow strings coming from its top and an elaborate red wrap around his torso. In warrior school, she had learned to identify other animals and was taught that porcupines were "far more superior" than other creatures. Still, other than Mikey, she never interacted with one in real life.

"What in the world?!?" Mattie exclaimed. She instinctively got up and ran in the opposite direction, slamming straight into what seemed like a gigantic, solid black net. She collapsed to the ground.

"Relax, take it easy," said the monkey with his face over hers.

Mattie could not believe what she was seeing. *Why would a monkey have anything covering his nakedness? What was happening?*

He then swung on the net's straight, solid parts and helped her up.

"Am I dead?" she asked.

The monkey laughed heartily. "Far from it. If you ask me, you're closer to heaven."

She scratched her head, confused. "Are we inside some giant net?"

"No, this is your new home!" he said theatrically.

Mattie looked for a way out in every direction and inquired perceptively, "Then why do I feel trapped?"

The monkey chuckled, "Well, technically, it's a cage, but it's also where we live."

"You're a monkey, correct?" she asked.

"And proud of it." He nodded emphatically.

I guess all animals are proud to be what they are, Mattie thought.

Then she asked, "Then why do you live here? And why do you have those red things covering you?"

He took the circular object off his head and put it on her head.

As her head was bigger than his, he tilted it completely to one side. It looked tiny on Mattie, but he still puckered his lips whispering pompously, "Not bad. My fez hat looks pretty good on you."

She reached her paw up and took it off, feeling uncomfortable with the covering. She handed it back to him asking, "It's called a fez hat?"

"Yep," he uttered, playfully juggling it between his hands and putting it back on his head.

Then, he put his hands on the red wrap that covered his chest. "And this is my beloved vest. It even has pockets!"

He opened up the wrap to show off a well-worn, red carved wooden stick inside.

"What's that?" Mattie asked, pointing at the wooden stick.

He grinned. "It's a drumstick and my most prized possession. Any other questions?"

"Tons. Why in the heck am I here?" Mattie asked.

"Wow, you mean you don't know?! You have the privilege of being the legendary Circus Planet's newest act. We're one of the best attractions this side of the Mississippi," the monkey declared with his chest held high.

Mattie looked around and saw an elaborate, vibrant red fabric above them with a flap nearby revealing the sun reflecting on the black, shiny surface surrounding them outside. It was similar to the one the blue rectangular beast had barreled down when she had been grabbed by the ape-like creature. Though the black surface seemed extremely flat and plain, unlike the wilderness.

"What's with all the rectangles, lines, and neat circles everywhere?" Mattie asked.

The monkey explained that the humans were obsessed with efficiency and order. They pave this black, shiny surface called a road that quickly gets them to other places, though it destroys the wilderness. And their primary goal, in everything they build and do, is to get a lot more of this small, rectangular, super-thin wood-like material and little, shiny rocks that are uncannily uniform in shape.

"They're always in a hurry to get more of it. The humans call it money, but I tried eating it once and it's nasty. Can't understand why they're so hungry for it," the monkey mused, shaking his head.

"So, they consume it?" Mattie asked.

The monkey replied, "I would assume so, though they never do it while we're looking. I mean, why else would they be so obsessed with accumulating it if it wasn't delicious, right?"

"That's what those big creatures with two feet are called? The humans?" said Mattie, quickly putting the pieces together.

He went on to explain that the humans ran the circus by teaching the animals to perform tricks in front of other humans who in turn, gave the circus humans money. The animals could understand everything the humans were saying though they weren't as evolved in their ability to understand the animal language.

"That's strange that we can understand the humans, given how primitive they are. They can't understand us at all?" said Mattie.

"Oh no, they're far too dumb. All they hear are noises when we talk, and we pretend not to be able to understand them either or else they'd boss us around even more than they already do. Though I have to give them credit for how they run this place. While they amass more of this money, they also keep us sheltered and well-fed with three square meals a day," the monkey replied.

"Why do they need me, then?" Mattie asked.

"Why, you're our latest moneymaker." He reached out his hand. "Sorry, I never introduced myself. I'm Christian. What's your name? And, I don't mean to be rude but what exactly are you?"

"I'm Mattie, a spineless porcupine," she answered, sheepishly,

"You mean you were born that way? You didn't attack a bulldog?" Christian asked.

"Nope, always been this way," Mattie said, shaking her head.

She expected Christian to be repelled but instead he shouted, "Cool! Can I give you a high five? I can tell everyone I touched a porcupine and lived!"

He held up his hand toward her. Mattie was visibly confused. He grabbed her paw, slapped it against his hand, and smiled. She was instantly reminded of all the times Mikey used to tap her paw after they had built a trap together. She felt a pang of guilt as she whispered, "I miss you, my high-five buddy."

13

ALL HAIL TO THE COMMANDER

MATTIE AND CHRISTIAN BECAME FAST FRIENDS. HE came from a long line of circus performers but was separated from his parents when he was young and transplanted here. He didn't remember much about them.

Christian was popular among the other animals and he considered them his family. He would often tell Mattie and the other animals about the fascinating history of circuses and how lucky they all were to be animals under the big, red tent. "We're the 'chosen ones.' I mean, where else do you not have to worry about predators? Plus, all your meals are hand-delivered to you by the humans!" Christian said. "Who needs the wild when all you have to do is perform a few tricks and you're set for life?"

He explained that Sirk, the main human who ran the circus, was the ringmaster and owner. "As long as you follow his orders," the monkey said, "he's a saint."

"Oh, so he's our commander," Mattie said.

Christian nodded and said, "Yeah, I guess. The main point is, don't upset him and keep him happy."

"So exactly like a commander then," Mattie said, thinking about her cruel father. She did wonder if she could somehow win over this new commander and start anew. To do so, she paid close attention to Christian's advice.

Christian often boasted that he was a ringmaster in training because he got to sit on Sirk's shoulder during training sessions. But given that bears and elephants can't sit on a human's shoulder, Mattie wondered how true it could be. She never questioned him about it because she could tell the distinction was vitally important to him.

From then on, Christian introduced Mattie as the world's only spineless porcupine. She did not like being associated with what she lacked but the other animals would "ooh" and "ahh" when he said it. And it felt good when others were in awe of her. At least it was better than the rejection she had experienced among her clan. After a while, she noticed Christian referred to all of the animals by their unique characteristics or talents: George, the black bear who could juggle with his left hand; Nelson, the elephant who could balance on a red ball; or himself—the monkey who could play drums.

During the initial days of Mattie's arrival, she noticed a few cages in the shadows, far from all the others. *Who was in there?* Mattie never saw any of them come out of their cages. They remained hidden in the darkness. Christian never mentioned any other animals. Finally, curiosity got the better of Mattie and she asked him.

"Yeah, that's where they keep Pearson. Sirk likes to keep him separate because he's not tame like the rest of us. He was captured in the wild a couple years ago and was a headliner at one time but eventually became defiant. Sirk's trying to break him into circus life so he can be a moneymaker again. We tried to talk to Pearson when he first arrived, but he just ignored us. I guess he thinks he's better than us, but he'll figure it out," said Christian.

"But what is he?" Mattie asked.

"We don't know," Christian replied.

Mattie's eyes widened and chills went down her spine. "Sounds scary," she said.

"Maybe that's another reason why Sirk keeps him separate from us. We're too valuable to become some predator's dessert," said Christian.

She gulped and quickly scurried in the opposite direction of Pearson's dark corner.

14

INTRODUCING JUNIPER,
THE NAKED PORCUPINE

ONE MORNING, MATTIE AWOKE ON A TABLE IN A heavily sedated daze. Sirk and another human prodded her with some metal instruments. She tried to move but it was hopeless. Terrified, she cried out, "Mama!"

The other human listened intently to her squeak and used a magnifying glass to study her face. He said, "Nope, not a mole-rat."

"Is it a hairless possum?" asked Sirk. The other human shook his head.

Mattie slurred, "I'm a spineless porcupine, you idiots!" but all they heard was more squeaking.

"How about a vole?" Sirk said.

"No. Too big."

"Hedgehog?" Sirk said.

"No, she's too big but she resembles a … oh my goodness. I think she's a naked porcupine!" the other human exclaimed.

"Finally!" Mattie said, but her voice was garbled.

Sirk hugged the human and shouted, "Boy, I hit the jackpot! She could be the star of our new show!"

Christian rode shotgun on Sirk's shoulder as the ringmaster brought Mattie into the ring and taught her tricks. She learned how to balance on a big ball, ride a skateboard, and do somersaults. Mattie was always a fast learner, and Sirk rewarded her with special treats like strawberries whenever she mastered a trick. It gave her a tangible sense of accomplishment. Plus, she knew strawberries were Christian's favorite, which made it even sweeter to her—as if she was surpassing her mentor. To Christian's annoyance, she often practiced somersaults in the cage late into the night until she passed out from exhaustion.

The night finally arrived for Mattie's debut. It was chaotic backstage, and she could hear a lot of hustle and bustle just beyond the curtain. Strangely though, she was the only one without a costume. She looked around and noticed the bears had birthday hats or top hats, and the elephants' backs were draped in red fabric saddles. Christian was wearing a dazzling red show vest and a hat with sparkles. Once again, she was the odd one out. She wanted to ask Christian if she could borrow one of his hats. That's when the gruff human stagehand named Oliver grabbed her and put her on a skateboard near the red curtain. On the other side, she could hear Sirk's voice booming.

"Ladies and gentlemen, boys and girls, welcome to Circus Planet, the longest-running stationary circus this side of the Mississippi. Tonight is a very special night. For the first time in the history of circuses, we have an animal that has never been seen before and will likely never be seen again. Introducing Juniper, the naked porcupine!"

"Juniper? But that's not my name," Mattie said. Oliver lifted the curtain and shoved the skateboard with her on it toward the stage. The lights were blaring. Disoriented, Mattie did everything she could to stay balanced on the zooming skateboard. Sirk enthusiastically swooped her up as the sound of applause and wonder filled the tent.

She performed her routine with Sirk, just as they practiced countless times. But there was one difference. Every time she did a trick, like balancing on a ball or completing a somersault, the humans cheered uproariously. Even the handful of bats that would stray into the top of the tent seemed to squeak with approval—though they still gave her the heebie-jeebies.

After her performance, Oliver ushered her backstage. He placed her back in the cage and quickly rolled a strawberry toward her, covering it in grime. Then he grabbed Christian.

"Good luck!" Mattie shouted to Christian.

"I don't need luck. I've done this millions of times," he said.

Mattie smiled broadly as she listened intently to the cheers of the crowd. It gave her a high and sent warm fuzzies all over her body. She loved the affirmation. Mattie munched on the soiled strawberry, too ecstatic and filled with purpose to taste the filth or care that somehow her name had become Juniper. *It's not like the name, Madeline, really fits me ... I'm not a warrior*, she thought. She was now a performer willing to do anything for the rush of amusing the audience.

15

THE MAIN ATTRACTION

NOT LONG AFTER HER DEBUT, MATTIE BECAME CIRCUS Planet's featured headliner. Sirk included her in more of the acts. She was harnessed into a custom-built saddle on Nelson, the elephant, as he stomped his way around the ring. The scary part was when Sirk would prompt Nelson to balance on his two hind legs and she would have to hold on tight. To alleviate her fears, Mattie often imagined her porcupine family in the crowd—Mom, Dad, Jasmine, and Trevor. They were all in awe of her as she rode high above them on an elephant. They could not touch her; she was finally safe and protected.

Tickets sold out every night. The humans could not get enough of Juniper, the Naked Porcupine. And Mattie could not get enough of them. She would take notes on the ground of her cage after every performance. Mattie jotted down what caused the loudest reaction in the crowd so she could perfect those moves, even if it meant risking her life. For instance, she would pretend to almost fall off Nelson when he stood on his two hind legs but then recover when he was back on all fours. That's when she would stand on her two hind legs and when she settled back in the saddle,

Nelson would pretend to almost fall. Even though it was extremely dangerous to balance on her hind legs ten feet off the ground on a moving elephant, it was a total crowd pleaser and that's all that mattered to Mattie. Even more than her own safety and wellbeing.

Sirk built a photo booth for his new superstar with a sign over it that read, "Juniper, the World's First, and Only, Naked Porcupine." He charged five dollars for the humans to take pictures with her and selected from the audience only those who had thin, curvy frames and tinny voices. This was Mattie's favorite part of the evening. Sirk would cradle her like a baby and the humans would come close saying things like, "Ooh, she's so adorable!"

Then they would caress her, while Sirk pulled them closer, holding poses and smiles while other humans held rectangular boxes that would erratically flash, as bright as the sun, toward them. It felt so good. She loved the sensation of touch and the bright lights. For the first time in her life, she was thankful she had been born without quills.

Every morning, Mattie was the first to be fed. Sirk paid less and less attention to Christian and the others. Instead, he lavishly attended to Mattie who he affectionately nicknamed, "My big meal ticket."

Mattie grinned and mused, *Wait till Trevor gets a load of me now. I'm not a meal on wheels, I'm a 'big meal ticket.' Whatever that means.*

Then one day, while Sirk was training the other animals, he shooed Christian off his shoulder and placed Mattie there. She had finally arrived, she decided with a huge grin. All the struggle and pain up to this point paid off. She had found the place where she belonged, seated high above all the others.

That's when she finally saw Pearson. Oliver dragged the wild, albino creature out of his cage, using a chained leash and collar around Pearson's neck and a whip to get his point across. Pearson had such a regal, powerful, and beautiful presence even amidst such atrocious treatment. They could flog his body but not his spirit.

When he saw Mattie on Sirk's shoulder, he looked to the ground and shook his head with pity. Mattie reacted defensively. "Don't feel sorry for me. I'm not the one in chains being whipped!"

Pearson looked deeply into her eyes and replied tenderly, "You don't need chains when you're already a slave."

His words hit Mattie like a fist to her sensitive belly but came out as a howl to the oblivious Oliver, who began to whip Pearson for being too noisy. Mattie was glad someone shut him up. Even so, his words pierced her heart. Deep inside, she knew they were true. She was a slave to everyone's approval, and Pearson threatened the fragile scaffolding supporting her newfound sense of self-worth.

The majestic animal refused to follow Sirk's orders. The ringmaster snapped at such defiance. He angrily shooed Mattie off his shoulder, grabbed an electric prod nearby, and repeatedly struck Pearson with it. Mattie squealed while all the other animals just turned away. She stood there appalled to see this side of Sirk. All those nights he cradled her and taught her how to perform—he became somewhat of a surrogate father to her. This was betraying everything she had come to know of her ringmaster.

After the beating, Pearson just laid there. That's when Sirk yelled at Oliver to grab a bucket of water, which he poured all over Pearson and growled, "Don't you dare defy me again."

Mattie hated Pearson. She tossed and turned all night with Pearson's words echoing in her mind. She ruminated, *What does that stupid, furry albino know? Looks like they scared all the color out of him—pale freak of nature.* Mattie snickered at her own mockery of him, ignoring the irony that the same words had once been used against her.

Christian could hear Mattie giggling to herself as they were the only ones awake. He couldn't sleep that night either after being dethroned from his special place in the circus hierarchy. He immediately assumed that Mattie's amusement had to do with the glee of her newly acquired position on Sirk's shoulder. Christian grumbled softly, "We'll see who gets the last laugh."

16

THE SHOW MUST GO ON

DURING MATTIE'S HEADLINER PERFORMANCE THE following night, she still couldn't shake Pearson's evaluation of her as a slave. *But what other option is there than performing for everyone's delight and approval?* She was so distracted by her thoughts that while balancing on a ball in the bright spotlight, which she'd done plenty of times with ease, she somehow lost her balance and fell off, smacking hard onto the dirty floor.

She lost consciousness for a moment but then realized what had happened. She was mortified—not because she was hurt, but due to her greatest fear of disappointing the crowd. She did not even look to see if she was bleeding as she scanned the faces in the audience. Even though many faces were filled with shock or concern for her, Mattie didn't stop scanning until one look of scorn confirmed what she believed about herself—that no matter how hard she tried to cover it up, she would always be a failure underneath. She knew that look too well. It was the one imprinted in her memory when her father first greeted her out of the womb. In her dazed state, she could almost see and hear her father from the one mocking face saying, "You can't outrun the truth—you're a nobody."

Suddenly, Sirk grabbed Mattie and put her on his shoulder. He smiled to the crowd but underneath his breath snapped, "Get it together. The show revolves around you." Her heart dropped at the thought of letting down another father figure.

Ignoring the aching pain in both her body and heart, she put on a smile and powered through the rest of her routine. She stuffed it all down until she was alone in her cage—that was when the tears silently rolled down her cheeks.

She woke up at dawn the next morning to practice balancing on a ball to get her mind off her misstep and to make sure it never happened again. Christian came by and asked, "Are you OK? What's going on?"

Mattie shared with him how she thought she had seen her father the night before. Pretending to be genuinely concerned, Christian said, "Oh my, I think you hit your head pretty badly. You might need to have Sirk call the vet to look at you."

"What's a vet?" asked Mattie.

"A human that will help you perform better than ever," Christian told her with a sly grin.

What Christian said made sense, so she asked, "How do I do that?"

"Just go lie down in your cage and refuse to eat. They'll get the hint."

So, she went into her cage and didn't move, and eventually fell asleep. She woke up to Sirk poking her and saying, "Get up, it's time to rehearse. I don't want another repeat of last night."

Mattie felt weak, both from not eating and from feeling like a failure. It was as if a half-ton iron rod pinned her heart to the ground. She tried to muster the strength to get up, but she ended up stumbling toward Sirk.

"What's wrong with you? You sick?" asked Sirk, putting two fingers on her tiny forehead to gauge her temperature. She looked up at him with her big brown eyes feeling exhilarated by his touch, though the sensation only lasted a moment.

"You are clammy," said Sirk as he left abruptly. When he returned, he was accompanied by the man who had prodded her with metal instruments when she first arrived. She was instantly filled with terror and thought, *Not him again!* She squealed and tried running away from him, but she was sluggish from exhaustion and starvation. She didn't get far before the man picked her up and began examining her.

After his observation, he said, "This could be due to her disorder. She might have a disease that we don't know about. It's hard to tell. I think it'll be best if I take her back to my lab so we can examine her more closely."

More humans like you poking and prodding me? No way! Mattie wiggled and squealed loudly. Sirk told the man, "I told you, unless you docs are willing to pay me twenty percent more than what I make from her every night, it's not happening."

Sirk grabbed Mattie. "All I need is for you to get her back to how she was … now!"

The man shook his head, then grabbed an IV and sedative from his bag, saying, "She won't perform tonight, but she should be better in the morning." As Sirk held Mattie still, the man administered the needle into her. Her eyes drooped, and she fell asleep.

Later she woke, disoriented. She saw Christian on the opposite corner of the cage, being his usual bubbly self, chatting it up with Nelson and the other animals. Slowly Mattie made her way toward them. Nelson asked, "Mattie, you OK? We saw the vet working on you yesterday."

"His name's not Vet. It's more like Threat," said Mattie. Nelson giggled a little. It warmed Mattie's heart to feel affirmed again. Though it had only been a couple days, she missed the thrill of entertaining an audience, large or small.

"What the heck was that thing he poked me with?" she asked.

"Was it sharp and shiny?" asked Christian.

She nodded her head. Christian looked away and changed the subject, "If you need more rest, it's fine. We can cover for you. It's just like old times. Right, Nelson?" Christian winked at the elephant who awkwardly gave a knowing smile.

Nelson recited the words Christian had coached him to say to Mattie, "Yup, Sirk still had the old sign featuring Christian, so he put it up and we did our old routine. The crowd liked the change-up."

Mattie's heart sank at the thought of being replaced so easily. But she was also curious about what the heck was coursing through her veins. Mattie played it cool. "Right on. So Christian, you never answered my question. What did he put in me?"

"Don't worry about it. When I got sick a few months ago, they put it in me as well. It made me wobbly and not think straight for a few weeks, but it'll help you in the long run. See, I'm all better!" Christian said. The peppy monkey then jumped, clicked his heels together, and took a bow saying, "Ta-da!" He started doing a jig and humming to himself gleefully. Nelson laughed.

Mattie started questioning her grasp on reality. Her legs felt like Jello and she wondered if they were wobbling like that during the entire conversation and she just happened to notice when Christian brought it up. Here, she could barely stand without shaking and Christian was practically doing the Cha-Cha around her. *Why am I even here? The circus is fine without me. Actually, it was probably better before I joined. Look how happy Christian and Nelson are now that they're back together. I don't belong here; I don't belong anywhere,* she thought.

17

THE BEGINNING OF THE END

MATTIE BECAME DESPONDENT, FEELING AS IF SHE WAS losing her sanity. She was weak, confused, and didn't have the strength to perform. She didn't know if it was from the vet's sharp and shiny object that was being put in her daily or her heavy heart. For fear of Mattie spreading an infection, Sirk placed her in a dark cage away from the active performers. She felt even more isolated, abandoned, and delirious. The first morning Mattie was in the dark cage—just when she thought she was completely alone, she heard a soft growl from the cell next to her.

"Who's there?" yelped Mattie, trembling.

"I'm Pearson. And you are?"

"Mattie," she replied.

"So that's your real name? I never thought Juniper fit you any way," said Pearson with warmth.

"How would you know? You don't even know me," Mattie barked.

The albino creature leaned toward her and said, "I've been observing you for a while now, Mattie. I was filled with despair watching all the animals here in the thrall of the ringmaster, completely blinded to how we're just a commodity to him. But you're different. I could see that you struggled when I mentioned that you were a slave. You knew it was true. This isn't you. No matter how many tricks you've tackled, it's never enough and you know there's more. Your heart's tugging at you, just like mine does. We need to get out of here."

"Wait a minute, where the heck am I anyway?" Mattie asked, confused.

"Mattie, you're where those who no longer perform go … tossed aside."

"But I can still perform! Get me out of here!" Mattie shouted and shook the bars. She did a somersault to prove she was still capable.

Pearson shook his head, "What are you doing?"

"Performing. It's why we're here, right?" Mattie replied.

Raising his left eyebrow, Pearson said, "You really believe that?"

"What else is there?" she asked, annoyed.

Pearson pointed toward the flap where the sun rays were peeking through, lighting up their gloomy corner and said, "A whole world exists outside the circus. Have you forgotten where you came from?"

"I have no interest in going back out there. I get three square meals daily, I have a tent over my head and a safe place to sleep. What else is there to ask for? Plus, my family is here." Mattie said.

Slowly Pearson moved toward her and in a gentle tone asked, "You think they're your family? Have they tried to check in on you?"

Mattie was quiet. After a few moments, Pearson moved closer, "Sirk and Christian have all the other animals brainwashed, but deep down your heart knows the truth. This is not your home."

Pearson saw sadness and fear on Mattie's face as the truth of what he said sunk in. She couldn't run from the fact that no matter how hard she tried or how well she performed, Mattie never felt good enough. She never felt like she belonged. Treading lightly, Pearson drew close to the bars between them. He was silent long enough to hear the light pitter-patter from Mattie's tears hitting the cage floor.

While Mattie's eyes were closed, he reached his right front leg through the bars, turned his paw upward to avoid hurting her, then tenderly caressed her back. She initially jumped away at his touch. But when she saw the compassion in his eyes, it reminded her of when her mom had removed all of her own spines in order to hold Mattie. Mattie felt eased.

After a while, she asked, "What do you want from me?"

Pearson responded with another question, "Why do you assume I want something?"

"Because that's the way the world works. Everyone wants something. Whether our family wants us to make them proud or our friends want us to ease their loneliness. The other performers want us to make them look good or the ringmaster wants to make the show a success."

Pearson put the back of his paw gently on Mattie's cheek and said, "Oh Mattie, you see so much but you refuse to do anything about it. Aren't you tired of living according to what others want?"

"It's all I know," Mattie said.

Pearson caressed her face again and said, "I spent my entire life trying to earn everyone's acceptance. My parents loved me but once they passed, I had no one to shelter me from rejection. I eventually ran away and got captured after the love of my life, Hannah, didn't want to start a family with me. All she could see was my white fur, and she didn't want our kids to grow up with the same stigma. But we can't run and hide from our pain forever."

Mattie's heart melted. She knew exactly what it was like to be rejected based on something that was completely out of your control. But then she pulled away, afraid of being taken advantage of in her vulnerability. Mattie growled, "And why should I trust you?"

"You're right. Don't listen to me. Listen to your heart. Ask yourself, do you really want to keep living this way? I'm not interested in hearing about what others want for you. What do you want?" asked Pearson.

Just thinking of going back to the treadmill to either constantly build new traps, learn new tricks, or perform for different crowds every night exhausted Mattie. "I'm tired."

"You have nothing to prove. That's all an illusion."

"How do you know?"

"I'm not banished to this corner because I can't perform. It's because I decided that my worth doesn't need to be proved. There's nothing worse than betraying yourself for the approval of others, so I decided to stop doing it," Pearson said.

This was a completely foreign concept to Mattie. Pearson continued, "It isn't love if you have to perform for it. It isn't acceptance if you have to pretend for it. We exist on this planet for love and acceptance. It's more vital than the air we breathe. You long for belonging, just as I do. And the good news is that even though we might not have gotten that from our own flesh and blood, we can become family with those whose hearts resonate with ours and we can heal together. Mattie, you've caused my heart to come alive again in this dark place, which is why I want to help you."

Mattie couldn't deny that her heart began to burn whenever Pearson spoke. But whenever her mind tried to imagine a life without having to perform and pretend, all she saw was a future shrouded in darkness and she cringed. The truth was, Mattie had no clue what she wanted anymore. She had become so accustomed to reading what others wanted and to pleasing them that she had forgotten how to read and satisfy her own heart. The thought of returning to herself overwhelmed her.

"Stop putting fantasies in my head. This is all there is to life!" Mattie yelled.

Pearson was quiet. Mattie eventually fell asleep with tears streaming down her cheeks. Pearson stayed awake watching over her protectively, knowing she was fragile. She was starting to transition—though her body slumbered, her heart was awakening.

18

I'M BEAT

MATTIE AWOKE TO SIRK GRABBING HER OUT OF THE cage as Pearson growled fiercely at him through the bars. Sirk thrashed his whip at Pearson but, to Mattie's surprise, the albino animal remained fearlessly defiant. *Why does he not fear for his life?*

Sirk yelled at Pearson, "Yeah, keep that up. I'm sure I can sell you off for your meat. That's about the only benefit you can provide me at this point."

Mattie was shocked at how easily Sirk was able to turn on a former circus headliner. Was she next to be sold for her meat? Maybe they were all just commodities to Sirk, bought and sold for the highest dollar, dead or alive. This thought shook Mattie to the core as Sirk set her on his shoulder and walked her back to the other performers. Though she once coveted being in this esteemed place, now she couldn't wait for him to set her down where she could feel the solid ground beneath her again.

But was anything steady for her these days? Everything seemed to be in flux and there was no security in what she once considered her family and home. Who she feared most under the big top, Pearson, seemed to be the only one who cared. Those she literally trusted with her life in every performance, Sirk and the other circus animals, seemed to only want her for her tricks. It was all so confusing. Up had become down, black had become white, and good now seemed evil. Mattie questioned if she truly wanted to stay in the circus even though she once could not have imagined leaving. All she had wanted was to be admired for who she was and to be cheered on by the crowds, but it was costing her very soul. Mattie thought she had arrived at true acceptance, but it was like every other group—accepting prospective members on the conditions of the three P's: performance, productivity, and perfectionism. She was sick of the circus and wanted out.

Sirk set her down with the other animals. They were especially chatty this morning. Christian swung toward her and gave her a big hug. Mattie involuntarily pulled back and immediately felt guilty. *Why would I pull back from my friend like that? He's always helping me and looking out for me. Pearson's wrong about him.* So, she drew herself into his hug though she no longer felt comfortable with his closeness.

"Welcome back! So how was quarantine land?" said Christian.

"Is that where I was?" Mattie asked.

Christian nodded and said, "We missed you. But thankfully, Nelson and I were able to hold things down and we're now averaging larger crowds without you!"

Mattie felt a pang in her heart but not as intensely as she had before. While she wondered why that was the case, Sirk came by and growled to his grumpy stagehand, Oliver, "Let's see if Juniper will take to Christian's drums. We gotta teach her something new 'cos no one's going to pay to see her do the same ol' tricks."

Quickly, Mattie turned toward Christian to see his reaction, knowing how important it was to him to be the only drummer under the big top. Christian's suspected insecurity was confirmed by the pale, sour look on his face. But he quickly shook it off and smiled, proclaiming with feigned enthusiasm, "Great, I get to teach you the drums!"

Mattie took swiftly to the instrument, being the fast learner that she was, and soon began performing once again to sold-out crowds, just as before. But somehow, it just wasn't as fulfilling. Christian now took over her old tricks as she performed drum solos to enthralled audiences—some even came from out of state to see her. They would hold up thin rectangular devices in front of their glowing faces, which she thought to be strange because they wouldn't be able to see her performance as clearly with the devices blocking their eyes. *The humans are so bizarre and captivated by boxes.*

Sirk was once again enamored with Mattie, often carrying her on his shoulder every chance he got. She was even with him when he guided a crew that used tar to put up a towering new sign across the big top's entrance, "The Legendary Circus Planet: Home of Juniper, the Naked Porcupine Drummer."

The sign irked her since it was the stage name and not her own that was becoming known. *That's probably why all the praise rings hollow*, she thought. Every morning, she felt like she was starting at square one in needing to prove herself. She fantasized that maybe if she only crossed out Juniper and put Mattie on the sign, the growing emptiness she couldn't shake would go away.

Meanwhile, she sensed Christian's envy reaching a fever pitch. During one drum lesson where she quickly picked up a new beat he was teaching her, Christian said, "Well, aren't you the Rockstar?" Mattie shrugged her shoulders.

Christian continued, "You know, you don't seem very grateful for the ways I've mentored you."

"I'm happy to help you with your tricks as well. That way, we can all succeed together," Mattie countered.

Christian slammed his drumsticks down and barked, "Well, it looks like the student has now become the teacher. Have you forgotten? You were nothing before you met me. I made you who you are."

"Don't be like this, Christian. You're like family to me. If it were up to me, I would want all of us to be headliners," Mattie replied.

"Whatever," the monkey sneered as he turned his back on her, put his hand up to signal he's heard enough, and promptly scurried off.

During one performance to a packed-out tent, a human with a bright light and what looked like a giant black eyeball mounted on another rectangle was pointed at her, following her every move. It began to feel like too much attention, which she never used to believe was possible.

Meanwhile, Sirk cut the other circus animals' performance time in half to make more room for Mattie's drum act. Christian began holding secret meetings with the other animals behind Mattie's back. "We need to do something. At this rate, some of us might be permanently removed from the show because of Mattie," he said.

As they discussed ideas on what to do, Christian turned to his right and saw a small can of tar that was used for mounting the new sign. He had a sudden flash of inspiration and asked Nelson to create a distraction with some loud trumpeting so he could sneak over and grab it. While Nelson was causing a commotion, Christian swung briskly over to grab the can and hid it in his cage.

Christian opened the can and the animals peaked in to catch a glimpse. It was black and sticky, so he asked George if he'd be willing to put a little on himself. After all, he was a black bear and could most easily conceal the substance. "We just want to make sure it doesn't harm Mattie," Christian explained.

Out of concern for Mattie, George put a tiny drop on himself and it immediately caused his fur to glue together. He jumped back and tried to shake it off but without success. George said, "We can't do this to her."

"Look, you're still alive. Seems like it only harms fur and Mattie doesn't have any so we're good," replied Christian.

The animals didn't feel good about it and protested. But Christian begged, with tears in his eyes, "If we don't do anything, we're not going to remain a family." He became quiet and reticent. A tear fell from his eye as he confessed, "I never told you the reason why I got separated from my parents when I was only ten months old. It was because there was a tiger that joined our circus that quickly became our star performer. There just wasn't enough food to keep all of us around and since I wasn't old enough to learn tricks, I was one of the first to go. All I have to remember them by is this." Christian pulled out the red beat-up little toy drumstick from a pocket inside his red vest.

George approached the despondent monkey and put his hand on his shoulder. Christian leaned into George as he confessed to all of them, "I just don't want to lose my family again."

19

TARRED AND FURRED

MATTIE WAS FAST ASLEEP. UNDER THE COVER OF darkness, George and Nelson kept a careful watch for the humans while Christian snuck close to her. He gently poured the tar all over Mattie's body. He made sure not to cover her face, for risk of killing her. The deal the circus animals had made for supporting Christian's plan was that no permanent harm would come to her body. What they didn't take into account was how this might scar her soul.

The next day Mattie awoke to discover the horrible thick black substance covering her from neck to toe. Everything she touched stuck to her including the dirt beneath her— she felt so filthy. Mattie made the mistake of touching her face, which left a black mark on her cheek. She felt even more repulsive, painfully reminded of Jasmine covering her with her quills.

Mattie saw a trail of tar leading back to Christian's cage. *My family always betrays me,* she thought, weeping. Mattie's squeals were so loud that everyone under the big top heard her, including Sirk and Pearson. Sirk rushed over, horrified to see her covered in tar. He opened her cage to get a closer look and gasped, taking a step back.

He screamed at her, "What did you do to yourself?" and promptly ran away to grab his phone, forgetting to shut her cage. This only confirmed her fear of now being utterly revolting and that it was all her fault. She wondered if she might have sleepwalked her way into the awful substance even though clear evidence suggested otherwise. It made twisted sense to her, given the experience reflected how she had felt about herself all along—she was an utter, murky mess. Maybe her subconscious was making her feelings of shame an external reality. She loathed herself, and once again, she took on the blame that laid squarely with another, just as she had with Jasmine's treacherous act.

Mattie wondered who Sirk might be calling. *An exterminator because she was beyond repair? At this point, did it matter to go on living?* She was OK with being put out of her misery because nothing seemed to matter anymore. Her blood family had betrayed her, her circus family was nowhere to be found in this moment of desperate need, and the only thing she knew how to do well, performing, no longer held meaning and significance for her. The emptiness she felt permeated deep into her bones, and the sticky substance weighed heavily on her skin.

A loud ruckus erupted on the other side of the tent. As soon as Pearson had heard Mattie's cry, he started banging wildly against his cage. When the stagehand, Oliver, checked on him, Pearson whimpered, lying on the ground as if wounded. Oliver grumbled, "What's wrong with you?"

Pearson simply responded with the warmest puppy-dog eyes begging for help. Oliver's simple heart melted, and he opened Pearson's cage to investigate. But as soon as he opened it and walked toward the seemingly injured animal, Pearson took off between his legs and headed straight for Mattie. Mattie could barely see through her swollen teary eyes when Pearson rushed toward her, grabbed her with his mouth, and sprinted out of the open circus flap and into the wilderness.

PART III:

THE WILDERNESS

20

A WILD MESS OF WILDFLOWERS

THEY ESCAPED INTO A DENSE MEADOW OF TALL wildflowers nearby. When Pearson could no longer hear the shouts of Sirk, Oliver, and the other stagehands who chased them, he let Mattie down.

Still covered in tar, Mattie now had patches of Pearson's fur attached to her where they had come into contact during the unruly escape. She saw and touched the fur that was now glued to her, fascinated. She said, "So this is how it feels not to be naked."

As awful as it was being covered in tar, she actually enjoyed the feeling of soft fur against her skin. At least it wasn't prickly, which was the sensation she was acquainted with growing up around porcupines.

Suddenly, they heard a truck engine roaring toward them. Sirk shouted, "I see them over there!" Sirk and Oliver barreled through the gorgeous meadow in their direction. Mattie squeaked in terror. Pearson scanned the horizon and saw a dense forest of oak trees nearby. He grabbed Mattie with his mouth and bolted toward it. The flowers provided good cover since they were taller than Mattie and Pearson.

While Mattie hung from Pearson's mouth, multi-colored petals stuck to parts of her still exposed tar-covered skin.

Sirk and Oliver were hot on their trail. When they reached the forest, Pearson dodged left just in time to get her out of the four-wheeler's path. While the truck was circling back toward them, Pearson climbed high up into a towering tree, still carrying Mattie. Panting from their near recapture, they hid among the lush leaves that seemed to wrap around them like a cocoon. Pearson sat Mattie down, quietly whispering, "sorry," to the tree as he caressed it, and then broke off a branch. When Sirk and Oliver got out of the truck to see where the paw tracks went, Pearson threw the branch far into the forest. Oliver heard the branch fall and shouted, "They're over there!"

Pearson encouraged Mattie to slow her breathing as Sirk and Oliver scoured the far section of the forest. The wily albino animal gently tore off leaves and wrapped his feet in them. Then he dropped down to smother their tracks before returning to the tree.

The two men continued to search the forest, trying to trace tracks but found nothing. Sirk shouted, "Juniper, come back. I ran off to call the vet for you. He can remove the tar."

Mattie looked at herself covered in a wild mess of fur and flower petals. It was very tempting to be cleaned up and back to a familiar world. *Sure, maybe she was betrayed and treated poorly, but who knew what lay beyond the horizon for her? Pearson could just be keeping her around as a snack in case he couldn't find food. After all, Christian did say that maybe the reason Pearson had been separated from the other animals was that they were too valuable to become some predator's dessert. Heck, she didn't even know what kind of animal he was. How could she trust him? Plus, he talks to trees!* However, she couldn't deny that her heart burned whenever he spoke. He seemed to be the only one who cared about what she wanted.

This debate raged within her so fiercely that she began to make her way out of the leaves. Pearson looked into her eyes with a tender yet intense gaze. "But you're not Juniper," he said.

This snapped Mattie back into the present. She was among the trees, her childhood home. She remembered all the time she had spent in treetops helping her mom gather twigs for their home and then scouting and setting up trap locations with Mikey.

"This is more of a home than anywhere else I've been," Mattie said. She reflected on her time at the circus and how no matter how good it had been, she had always felt like it wasn't for her. Mattie never felt good enough. Something was missing, and now she realized why. They never knew Mattie—only Juniper, the performer.

Sirk sighed in frustration and headed toward the truck. He growled at Oliver, "You have thirty days to find replacements that are just as good or you're fired!"

Pearson shook his head in disbelief. Mattie thought, *Wow, I didn't realize I was so easy to replace.* At that moment, she realized, no matter what lay before her and Pearson in the wilderness, she could not return to performing for an audience and a master who only saw her as being as good as her last trick.

21

THE FOREST AMONG THE TREES

PEARSON THOUGHT IT WAS A GOOD IDEA TO STAY IN THE tree for a few days in case Sirk and Oliver got desperate and widened their search for them to neighboring lands. They wouldn't be able to outrun the truck. The tar on Mattie had begun to harden, which made it difficult to both move and remove. "The owls will know how to get it off," Pearson said. He turned toward the tree and asked, "Have you seen the owls?"

Mattie shook her head and asked, "Why are you talking to the tree?"

Pearson motioned her to be silent and whispered, "Listen. They talk slowly. You need to slow down to hear it."

Curious, she slowed down her breathing. It was quiet for a while, which gave Mattie enough time to wonder again if Pearson might be a lunatic and whether escaping with him was a big mistake.

She whispered to Pearson, "Ummm, I don't think trees can talk."

"Just because you haven't heard them speak yet doesn't mean that they don't. It means you weren't patient enough to listen. After I ran away, I spent many nights among the trees discovering that those creaks weren't just noises," Pearson said quietly.

Then came a very low groan and rumble from the base of the tree. It sounded like, "There." The branch in front of them slowly pointed toward the west. She suspected she might have mistaken the wind for the voice and the branch moving.

Pearson said, "Thank you," and graciously put his hand on the tree. He then turned to Mattie. "We need to rest. We have a long journey in front of us."

Mattie didn't need much convincing. After all, she thought she might be hallucinating about "talking trees." She was exhausted—first, the treadmill of building traps and performing tricks, to now carrying the heavy weight of the tar on her skin. She fell into a deep sleep lulled by the soft breeze that swirled through the leaves nestling her like a cocoon.

The leaves were still wrapped around Mattie when she awoke. As she lay there in a peaceful, meditative state, she listened to the birds chirping their jolly song. The sun's rays would occasionally peek through and warm her face as the leaves shading her danced to the capricious rhythm of the breeze. She looked around to see if Pearson was nearby, but she couldn't see him. Mattie figured he might be foraging for food.

As her breathing slowed, she could feel how painfully exhausted her body was. She was secretly grateful for being covered in tar because it gave her an excuse to rest. While gazing at the leaves interwoven with sunlight, she heard a low, slow voice whisper to her, "Listen to your body. It knows. Though your mind might tell you to keep moving, your body knows best. And it will tell you if you slow down and listen."

She was immediately reminded of Christian's hug and how her body wanted to pull away even though it didn't make sense to her. Her body knew before her mind did that Christian had malicious intentions toward her. The voice continued speaking, "You believe you are not enough."

Mattie recognized the voice from the day before. It was the one who told them where the owls were. But more importantly, the truth it spoke resonated to her core. This made sense given it was coming from a being connected to the ancient depths of the earth.

Mattie studied the tree intently since it seemed to be speaking to her. That's when she realized it was the tallest tree in the forest. She looked up and noticed that the branches toward the top were cracked and damaged due to their exposure to the wind and sun. She connected deeply with the tree and to how it suffered for being different from its surroundings. She knew exactly what it felt like to be exposed to the elements and thus, enduring more damage than others. Out of curiosity, she asked the tree, "How do you protect yourself?"

Mattie already knew how she protected herself, by learning new skills and tricks. But how does a tree protect itself from being different? The tree was quiet for some time before responding, "My roots protect me. They go deep as I am tall. The neighboring trees often try to steal water from my source since my roots go deeper than theirs. Their roots become entangled with mine and I need to break their hold by expanding my roots until there's no longer room for them. There's enough water for all of us, but some of them are lazy and just want to tap into my source when they see how lush I've become. They don't want to do the work for themselves of growing their own root system. They just want to piggyback off my hard work."

Mattie pondered the deep wisdom of this mature tree. The tree continued, "It might sound selfish that I don't let the other trees take from my source. I truly want them to prosper, but I will never become the blessing I am meant to be if I don't protect myself. As I flourish, all those around me benefit from the vast shade, bountiful fruit, and beauty I provide. But if I let the other trees take from me, no one benefits. I wither and they never learn to tap into their own source and become strong, mature trees like myself. There's enough water for all of us, but we each need to dig deep for ourselves. I hope to inspire them, but I can't do the work for them."

Mattie saw the connection between what the tree was saying and her time at the circus. Her success wasn't meant to take away from others but to inspire them to take their acts to the next level together. She felt that Christian was only interested in taking credit for her hard work instead of creating his own success. And when she wouldn't let him, he was filled with jealousy and accused her of being selfish and ungrateful. After all, in his mind, he had made her what she was.

Mattie began to see there was enough to go around for everyone. At that moment, as she looked around the dense forest, she realized there was plenty of sunshine, water, and lush soil for all. Some trees acted selfishly due to fear of an impoverished future that didn't even exist, causing them to greedily take from each other and hoard resources. However, it was a self-fulfilling prophecy created by the belief that there wasn't enough to go around. Ultimately, everyone loses when they play the zero-sum game. She hoped for a chance to see Christian again and share with him the wisdom of this bountiful tree.

After another nap, she awoke to the sun's last rays filtering through the cracked branches toward the treetop. The fickle iridescent sunset shone through the weathered sections of the tree like an intricate lattice. She looked at the other trees surrounding them. The sunset didn't glow like the one she was witnessing above her. The tree's "flaws" were what made the spectacle so breathtakingly unique. Even the bats that began circling above looked magical as evening crept in, though not enchanting enough for her to want them to come close—she shooed them away.

The tree spoke slowly to her, "I'm glad you are finally resting. When we think we're not worthy of love, we are constantly in motion, producing and perfecting ... terrified of the moment when we're actually still enough to discover whether we're loved for who we are or only for what we can give and do." The tree continued, "How much can a fruit control its efficiency, productivity, and growth other than to abide and be nourished by its roots?"

She reflected on the tree's roots and how they grow deep in the darkness, unseen. Yet they provided the nourishment needed to produce all that is visible—the beautiful trunk, fruit, branches, and leaves. What was the most vital part of the mighty oak? Its hidden labyrinth of roots. Without them, the tree would die.

She thought about her life and how maybe, like trees, what sustained her was not what could be seen and admired, but rather what was hidden from view. She had been so focused on making her "fruit" and "leaves" look good, but what about her roots? Maybe that was why she felt like she was going to topple over from exhaustion. With desperation, she said aloud, "What are my roots?"

After a long pause, the tree said, "Your true nature. When you cease performing, that's when you can connect with it and be continually nourished with its life."

Mattie said, "And what is that?"

She felt the leaves envelop her even more as the tree whispered gently, "What you've been running from your entire life—the warrior within you. Right now, she's scared and hurting. She needs to be comforted and loved ... to know she is enough."

Her mind impulsively raced through reasons to deny the revelation. "I haven't had a harder life than anyone else. Also, if I'm so frightened, why am I able to perform death-defying stunts on an almost nightly basis? I'm the star of Circus Planet!" she told the tree.

A long silence hung between them. Then Pearson came back with some wild strawberries for her to eat. He could tell that she was deeply disturbed because she barely noticed his arrival with her favorite treats. "You OK?"

Mattie snapped her head toward him, surprised by the lack of hyper-awareness that she usually had of her surroundings. She answered, "Ummm, either I was dreaming or the tree talked to me."

"What did the tree say?" asked Pearson.

She motioned for Pearson to come close with a tremendous amount of difficulty due to the tar, fur, and flower petals caked on her. As he leaned in, she whispered in his ear, "That it's time to go to see the owls and get this stuff off me." The truth was, she was too perturbed by what the tree had said to share it.

22

AN OWLING GOOD TIME

PEARSON GRACIOUSLY PUT HIS PAW ON THE TREE'S trunk to thank it for providing them shelter and guidance before maneuvering Mattie onto his back for the journey. The leaves of the tree seemed to wave and shimmer in the sunlight as they parted. Mattie heard the tree say, "Let go of who you think you should be and you will be free."

They traveled for days while Mattie mostly slept. When she was awake, she pondered the tree's words while also struggling with guilt for being immobile. It was debilitating not only to her body but to her heart to not be able to show off her abilities. While initially she had been secretly grateful for the tar, now she obsessed over how the owls would remove it. *Maybe they have a secret potion or tool,* she thought. She couldn't wait to be free of the tar that clung to her like ugly, black glue.

Mattie started plotting how to win the owls over to help her, despite being unable to move. Her usual way of shielding herself when she felt insecure in new interactions was to entertain and awe others with tricks, gifts, and jokes so they wouldn't see what she believed herself to be—a worthless reject. But Mattie couldn't drum or dance and wasn't feeling particularly funny. She could only use her words to impress them.

"What are the owls like?" said Mattie aloud.

"I haven't met them myself, but I hear they are very wise," said Pearson.

The first image that popped into Mattie's mind was a group of old, demure creatures leaning on canes. She decided she would employ intellectual banter to win their favor. Little did she know she was in for quite a surprise. Mattie was sleeping on Pearson's back when she heard uproarious laughter from the trees over them. She was convinced that they were surrounded by hyenas. She instinctively yelled, "We're under attack!"

The creatures laughed even harder when one of them said, "Honey, the only thing under attack is our eyes."

Another said, "What happened? Did nature throw up on you?"

Pearson tried not to join these mysterious creatures in cracking up but couldn't help it and started shaking from laughter with Mattie on his back. Mattie almost fell off; she was indignant. She yelled back at the creatures, "Who do you think you are? Do you even know who I am?"

One of the creatures flew down and landed right in front of Mattie. She was shocked to see a chubby owl staring her straight in the eyes for what seemed like ages. *Was he pondering deep wisdom to impart to her?* She dared not interrupt.

Then the rotund owl answered, "Nope. Don't know who you are," and playfully did a backflip off Pearson to the ground as the owls above burst into more laughter. Mattie was so confused. *What was happening?* Mattie's eyes told her that she was among the owls, but her brain did not compute the ludicrous scene happening in front of her. *Maybe I'm still dreaming,* she thought.

Pearson set Mattie down on the ground and respectfully

said, "Oh wise owls, we've traveled a long way for your help. This is Mattie and she's been covered in tar. Could you please help remove it?"

Three other owls hopped down from the trees and huddled in a circle with the facetious backflipping owl. There was a low hum of conversation and a few snickers. The tall owl casually offered, "Cool. I'm Dru. We have an idea, but it'll take some time. Why don't you hang out with us tonight?"

Mattie let out a sigh and Pearson said, "Yes, thank you from the bottom of our hearts."

Some of the owls giggled in surprise when Pearson used the word, "hearts." Dru said, "Don't thank us yet, but yes, we'll put our *hearts* into it." Then he winked at his parliament of buddies.

23

MESSY, COMPLICATED, AND BEAUTIFUL

THE HEAVY-SET OWL CAME OVER AND SET BLACKBERRIES and raspberries in front of Mattie and Pearson. "I know where all the best patches are," he boasted.

"Yeah, I can tell," Pearson said, chuckling.

Mattie nudged Pearson for fear of him offending the big owl but instead, the owl let out a belly laugh. "Touché." He then reached out toward Pearson, "I'm Pete. What's your name?"

Pearson grabbed his talon and shook it heartily. "I'm Pearson."

Pete looked at Mattie as he pointed at Pearson. "You got a good friend right there."

"What makes you say that?" Mattie asked. Suddenly, she realized she never really thought of Pearson that much or anyone else for that matter. She was too consumed with how she could further improve and fix herself. *Maybe I am trying to outrun the feeling of not being enough*, Mattie wondered, still haunted by what the tree had said to her.

Pete interrupted her thoughts, "Didn't he carry you all the way here to get this stuff off you?" Mattie had thought about that but figured he might have some ulterior motive, such as keeping her as a portable snack in case of emergency. Getting the gunk off her would make her a more delectable meal. Mattie shrugged her shoulders, though it kind of hurt to do that.

"Well, from where I'm standing, this albino fella is looking out for you. But what do I know? I'm just a silly owl," Pete said as he playfully tossed a raspberry into the air, caught it in his beak, and gulped loudly.

Pearson chuckled. "You're so not what I expected."

"And what was that?" Pete asked.

"An austere, genteel owl," chimed in Mattie.

"Oh, those are the stuffy ones further into the forest," Pete responded.

Confused, Mattie said, "Wait, then who are you?"

"We're the ones who realized that doing everything right and by the book wasn't fun," Pete declared.

Dru and the two other owls came over, all holding something behind their backs.

Mattie was too grateful to process what Pete just said. Instead, she was already fantasizing about what it would be like to be herself again. She could drum, dance, and put on a show to prove herself to these owls so they would treat her with respect, unlike how they were currently engaging with her. Nothing incensed her more than being belittled by others. It reminded her too much of her early days at warrior school when she was incessantly bullied by Jasmine, Trevor, and other insolent porcupines.

Dru said, "You need to close your eyes though."

Mattie didn't feel too thrilled about that, but she was way too eager to be rid of the tar. She closed her eyes. Then she felt each of the three owls come close and place something on her body. Then Pete said, "Wow, that's beautiful."

"Yippie, I must be my naked self again!" Mattie thought. But when she opened her eyes, she saw that each of the three owls had placed heart shapes formed from wood onto the

few still bare parts of her tar-covered body. The owls smiled with glee at their magnificent work and gave each other high fives.

One of the tall owls said, "Now that's a work of art, folks."

Immediately, Mattie had flashbacks to being teased in warrior school and never wanting to be the butt of a joke again. This was why she worked so incessantly to become popular and successful. Mattie could not restrain her anger any longer and screamed, "What about the freaking tar! Are you owls, idiots? WE ASKED YOU TO REMOVE THE TAR!"

Dru grinned, unfazed by her tantrum, and said, "Why remove something that's stunning? You wouldn't be a walking collage of fur, flowers, and hearts without it."

Another owl added, "Yeah, we wanted to give you a physical reminder that you are lovable even in your mess. Also, how else will you keep all the mementos from your journey? Bags are so annoying for us animals to carry, you know?"

In her blinding rage, triggered by the painful flashbacks, Mattie mistook their kind, playful words as invalidating, sarcastic taunts so she yelled, "Yes, give me a bag!"

The owls looked at each other and shrugged their shoulders. Dru said, "Sorry, we don't have bags. But maybe the otters do. They occasionally collect them from the river."

Pete chimed in, "They might even know how to remove the tar!"

"Where are the otters or are you too brainless to know?" Mattie muttered, grinding her teeth.

Surprised by Mattie's outbursts, Pete's eyes widened, and he pointed west toward the sunset.

Mattie motioned to Pearson to pick her up. "Let's go."

Dru turned to the other owls and said, "Well, I thought it was a nice gesture."

"But it's not what I asked you to do," barked Mattie.

The owls pondered her words and realized she was right. Dru was the first to speak up, "You're right. Even though our intentions were good, we should've asked for your permission first. I, for one, am sorry." The other owls nodded in agreement.

Pete said, "Yeah, please forgive us."

Mattie's anger melted in light of their apology. She responded, "I forgive you."

The owls grinned, then began playing soccer with a stone, and Pete motioned to Mattie. "We need a goalie."

Mattie rolled her eyes and couldn't help but laugh at the ridiculous nature of these owls. It dawned on her that they weren't disrespecting her, but they just saw everything in life as play as Pete had mentioned before she got sidetracked. It wasn't personal. They didn't take anything too seriously based on what she observed. As she pondered that, she realized it's not a bad way to live. Maybe they were wise after all.

She took a deep breath and decided it wasn't worth fighting these silly creatures anymore, so she might as well have a little fun with them. She nodded and said, "I'm very *goal-oriented*."

The owls squealed with delight. Dru and Pete made a makeshift goal around Mattie with a few branches. Then they made another goal on the opposite side and asked Pearson to be the other goalie, to his sheer delight. Dru and Pete were the team captains and they both gleefully fought over having Mattie as their goalie. She was shocked and asked, "Don't you want Pearson as your goalie? He can actually move."

Dru joked, "Nah, you're way better looking," then winked at Pearson who let out a hearty laugh.

After splitting into teams of two, they kicked the stone back and forth. With Pearson's nimble goal-keeping skills on their side and Mattie just standing immobile at her goal,

Pete's team quickly scored five goals. Mattie literally just watched the stone come toward her and only followed it with her eyes as it rolled right past her again and again.

Every time a goal was scored on Mattie, the owls and Pearson would roll on the ground laughing because it was so funny to watch her do nothing to stop the stone from going into the goal. She couldn't help but laugh along at the absurdity of her goal-tending skills, or more accurately, lack thereof.

After a while though, she grew tired from the heaviness of the tar and said, "As *heart-wrenching* as it is to not *kick* it with you anymore, I'm in a *sticky* situation that needs my attention."

The owls laughed, then went over and tried to high five her. They ended up just awkwardly patting her wooden heart adornments. Pete grinned at Mattie. "Hey, thanks for being a good sport. We're glad you finally came around."

Dru chimed in, "Isn't life more enjoyable when you're not taking it so seriously? But hey, we're just silly owls. What do we know?" Dru winked at Mattie.

Mattie thought about how her heart felt much lighter after playing with them. "Maybe you owls do know a thing or two, after all," she admitted to Dru. He then turned toward the owls and gave them a knowing grin and a nod. Mattie giggled and realized they knew what they were doing all along, teaching her a lesson that life is better when there was fun and laughter in the mix.

Mattie thanked the owls and motioned goodbye as best she could by wiggling her stiff body. Pearson then drew close to her, swung her onto his back, and carried her toward the river. On their way, Pearson said to Mattie, "You know, I really do think you're beautiful, mess and all." Misty-eyed, Mattie could tell his words were heartfelt. After a short pause, he continued, "I mean it. I know that you're messy and complicated, but that's what draws me toward you, not away from you."

Mattie pondered his words the rest of the way to the river. She never thought it was possible that anyone could love her when she was cranky and on top of that, completely immobile. She had nothing to contribute or attract him to her, yet this strange animal kept caring for her. But again, the wounds from her past betrayals led her to a darker conclusion, *I'm just a portable snack to him. As soon as I get this junk off me, I need to make my escape.*

24

HELLO FROM THE OTTER SIDE

BEFORE THEY EVEN ARRIVED AT THE RIVER, A YOUNG otter named Charlotte spied Pearson and Mattie coming over a sun-soaked hill. She ran to tell her family that she had seen the most uniquely beautiful creature covered in wooden hearts and flowers riding on a radiant white animal.

"You have the wildest imagination, Charlotte," said her mom, Wendy. She continued rationally, "There's no way that exists in real life though, sweetie."

Her brother, Richie, teased Charlotte, "Get your head out of the clouds and back in the river where it belongs."

Charlotte calmly baited Richie. "Care to wager five clams?"

"Sure, that'll be the easiest five clams I've ever made," Richie said.

That was when Pearson and Mattie passed through some brush and arrived at the river. Wendy and Richie's jaws dropped.

Charlotte smirked at Richie. "Five big, juicy ones, okay?"

"My goodness, they *are* stunning," Wendy exclaimed, in awe.

The otters meandered their way through the river toward Pearson and Mattie who were resting on the shore. Charlotte approached reverently as if they were A-list celebrities and stuck out her paw shyly. "I'm Charlotte."

Pearson shook Charlotte's paw. "Hi, Charlotte. I'm Pearson, and this is Mattie."

Mattie barely smiled, which is all she could manage with the tar now fully hardened. Still awestruck, Wendy came over muttering, "I don't mean to stare …"

Mattie's face turned downcast, expecting what Wendy would say next. But, to her surprise, Wendy said with amazement, "But you two are the most magnificent creatures I've ever seen."

Mattie's eyes widened and her heart filled with warmth. It had been a while since she had felt admiration from an audience, and she hadn't realized how much she missed it.

Mattie said, "Thank you, I really needed to hear that."

"The pleasure is all ours. I'm Wendy. How can we be of help?" Wendy said.

"My friend here, Mattie, needs to get this stuff off her," said Pearson.

Looking astonished, Wendy turned to Mattie and said, "You sure you want to remove all these gorgeous flowers and hearts?"

Mattie had never thought of the tar as a good thing. But now that the otters had pointed out how it embellished her with beauty, she was having second thoughts.

Mattie blurted out, "Well, how about we join you for dinner and I could think about it?"

Pearson gazed at Mattie with shock.

"Absolutely! What are you craving?" Wendy asked.

Mattie grinned. "Strawberries, if any are nearby."

Wendy turned toward Richie and Charlotte. "Make sure to get the best ones for our honored guests."

Excitedly they dove into the river, hopped to the other

shore, and through some bushes. Wendy continued staring at Mattie. "Sorry. I can't stop admiring how beautiful you are. I'll let you two get situated. We'll be back soon."

Wendy dove into the river and reached the other shore, then Pearson turned toward Mattie. "What's going on? Weren't you obsessed with getting the tar off yourself?"

"I'm having second thoughts," Mattie confessed.

"Why?" asked Pearson.

"I kind of like the anonymity of hiding behind all this. No one knows I'm a naked porcupine."

"True. But you can't move," Pearson replied.

"Well, beauty is pain," said Mattie and chuckled.

"It also fades. But it's up to you, Mattie," Pearson said tenderly.

The otter family returned with a bounty of strawberries.

"*Bon appétit*," Wendy said as she set the delectable berries before them.

Due to Mattie's limited movement, Pearson fed a few of them to her first before starting on them himself. Charlotte watched them in admiration and shyly asked, "Are you two a couple?"

Wendy turned toward Charlotte sternly. "Charlotte, that's rude."

Pearson chuckled. "It's OK. We are a couple of …" He took a long pause for effect. Charlotte nudged Richie to gloat over her, seemingly correct, perception of their relationship when Pearson continued, "friends if that's what you're asking."

"Yes, two clams for me!" Richie yelled excitedly while pumping his fist in victory.

Charlotte shook her head with a wry smile at her defeat.

25

BE PRESENT IN THE CURRENT

A FEW DAYS HAD PASSED SINCE MATTIE AND PEARSON
had set up camp with the otters by the river. Though Mattie
was starting to grow attached to her disguise as a new source
of identity, the immobility was beginning to wear on her.
Plus, the flowers were wilting and turning brown. The
rotting smell was suffocating her.

That night, during their usual dinner with the otter
family, Mattie shared with Wendy, "I'd like to get this stuff
off me."

"You sure?" Wendy asked. Mattie nodded.

Wendy went over to examine her and knocked on
various parts of the tar. "It sounds like a clamshell. My guess
is that removing it would be similar," Wendy said. "Let's
wait until morning when there's light and give it a shot."

Early the next morning, Wendy, Richie, and Charlotte
waded Mattie into the river to their usual clam-smashing
spot, surrounded by large rocks. The water swirled there,

outside the main current. Pearson remained right next to them on the shore, pacing anxiously and hoping that their plan would work.

Wendy grabbed a large rock and instructed her pups to do the same. When all three of them had large rocks, Wendy asked Mattie to stay calm pressed against the large rocks, chest-high in the river's water. But Mattie was anything but calm. She shivered in the water, terrified of her new otter friends unintentionally hurting her.

Wendy directed Richie and Charlotte, "OK, only one time and not too hard on the count of three. We need to see if it'll make a dent first."

Wendy, Richie, and Charlotte held the rocks high over their heads right above Mattie who closed her eyes tightly and clenched her body. Wendy counted, "One, two, three!"

The three otters slammed their rocks down on Mattie's tar-covered torso like it was a clamshell. "Crack!" echoed loudly among the hills. Pearson rushed into the river, toward Mattie, fearing the worst had happened.

"Are you OK?" said Pearson while cradling her shaking body.

Mattie peered out with one eye and with a trembling voice, said, "Eek, it's so cold."

She put her hand to her chest where there was a large crack in the tar. Water rushed into the crevice as she continued to shiver.

"Quick, let's peel off the tar!" Pearson shouted.

He and the otters picked at the opening and as they did, the current washed away the fur, flowers, and heart covered sections they were able to peel off. Mattie smiled as the exhilaration of feeling sensations again slowly returned to her body, piece by piece. The chilly water gliding over her naked skin rejuvenated her; it was as if she was experiencing her body anew. She wiggled her fingers and toes, maneuvered her head in circles, and stretched out her limbs in childlike wonder.

They removed most of the tar, but a few stubborn lumps remained. Wendy said, "Let's move her into the current. Its force should be able to take care of the rest."

"I'm not a good swimmer so I'll stay here," said Pearson.

"Wait, neither am I," Mattie admitted with concern as the otters waded her over toward the center of the river.

Before Mattie could further protest, Wendy turned toward Charlotte and Richie. "Hold her tightly. Two kicks to the right and we'll be there."

"Wait a second …" Mattie protested as they all moved quickly to the right.

Suddenly, a rush of water pressed against all of them mightily, carrying them quickly down the river. Mattie screamed as they rode the current like a wild roller coaster. There was no way out even if she tried—all she could do was trust the otters and let go.

When she did, she relaxed enough to feel her body. It almost seemed like time slowed down even though she was whizzing by her surroundings in the powerful river. Her breathing calmed, and it was as if she was seeing the world for the first time. The trees, the sky, orange poppies, and blackberry bushes alongside the river—it was all so vibrant. She could also feel the stubborn pieces peeling off her skin as tiny, tickling bubbles replaced them.

The world was magical. Mattie thought, *This is what life must be like when I'm not so busy trying to control it. While I've been so preoccupied with what's around the corner, I'm missing the greatest gift—the present moment that's continually being offered to me. Thankfully, I keep getting new chances to catch it.* She grinned with joy. The tar shell was like a cocoon shedding off of her and the river her place of metamorphosis.

Then Wendy yelled, "There are rocks ahead, kick four

times to the left!" And like a torpedo, all of them rushed left and exited the current. Slowly they made their way onto the riverbank.

Once they reached the shore, Mattie struggled to walk since she was still getting reacquainted with using her limbs again. Wendy came over to help her lie down on a sandy bank, then sat next to her. As they took their time to catch their breath, the pups played tag on the shore.

"All that boundless energy wasted on the young ..." Wendy said.

Mattie chuckled, then turned to look into Wendy's eyes. "Thank you. I feel reborn."

Wendy replied with a knowing smile, "The river has a way of doing that."

Mattie grinned back and nodded. They both turned and gazed in awe at the magnificent, shimmering river sweeping before them. Mattie asked, "How do you know where the current is? You knew exactly where it was and how to get in and out of it."

Pointing at the river, Mattie said, "It all looks like water to me."

Wendy laughed. "I've lived in this river my entire life. The only constant is that it's always changing. A branch that fell into the river miles away could completely shift the current in front of us. The only way to navigate it is to be completely present and find where the flow is *right now*."

Wendy motioned for Mattie to join her in closely observing the river's surface. She then pointed at the riverbank. "You see that flower over there and how it's moving?" Mattie looked and saw a small blue flower spinning in circles adjacent to a few roots on the river's shore.

"Now look toward the middle of the river from where that flower is. You'll notice how the flow changes from that reference point," Wendy explained as she drew an imaginary line from the flower toward the center of the river. Mattie looked intently and noticed a very slight change in the water's pattern from the flower toward the middle of the river. Wendy continued drawing imaginary lines. "I can find the current by referencing any object in the river because it's all connected. We're all at the mercy of its flow and must learn to navigate accordingly."

"Kind of like life," Mattie said, chuckling.

"Exactly." Wendy sang, "We couldn't control it even if we tried, so it's best to let go and enjoy the ride."

The mama otter put her paw on Mattie's shoulder and said, "That's a lullaby my mama used to sing to me. And now I pass it onto you, sweet Mattie." Maybe it was because she no longer had tar on her that Wendy's love sank deeply into her heart.

Mattie reflected on her journey thus far. The only constant was that it was unpredictable. Never could she have imagined that she would learn how to build traps from a spider, be a headlining performer in a circus, be covered with hearts by facetious owls, or receive a life-altering lesson from a wise otter. She also thought about all the pain from being rejected by her clan and her circus family and how she was now being taken care of by a mysterious albino animal whose agenda she still couldn't figure out. Mattie thought, *Nothing lasts, good or bad. So, it's best just to be open to what comes and goes.*

That was when Pearson galloped toward them panting. "Thank God, you're alive!" he shouted.

Mattie stood up and wobbled toward Pearson. She leaned in and embraced him for the first time. He was caught off guard by her unexpected affection and muttered, "What happened to you?"

"The river," she said and nuzzled her head into his chest. Pearson laughed.

"I know that." Pearson examined her body that was now virtually tar-free. He smiled.

"I have no idea why you're helping me, but thank you," she whispered tenderly to Pearson. A tear formed in his eye. He embraced her warmly in return and kissed her on her forehead.

26

SIGNIFICANT OTTERS

As they sat by the riverbank watching the sunrise, Mattie said to Pearson, "I have a confession to make."

He turned toward her and asked, "What's eating you?"

With a slight tremble in her voice, she said, "Well, funny thing is that I thought it would be you. This whole time I assumed you were keeping me around so you could eventually eat me."

Pearson was quiet for a while. "I get why you're suspicious of everyone. So many have hurt and betrayed you. It totally makes sense. And I should earn your trust. You're worthy of that. But the only reason I'd lick you would be to groom you. The only time I'd put you in my mouth would be to carry you out of harm's way."

Mattie's heart warmed and she smiled slightly. Pearson looked over and saw her smile. He then playfully licked Mattie all over and joked, "This is what you get for thinking I'd eat you."

Mattie giggled. "OK, enough. Eek, it feels so yucky! We porcupines don't do such grooming, for obvious reasons."

"Then how do you stay clean?" Pearson asked.

"Easy, we don't," she said, slightly annoyed.

Mattie then headed toward Wendy, Charlotte, and Richie who were preparing breakfast. Pearson hopped to her side and bumped her gleefully. He playfully covered his nose to tease her about not grooming. She tried to hold back her grin but couldn't. She bumped him back.

Pearson chewed a blackberry and maneuvered one of the seeds to the center of his mouth. "And this is for how many strawberries?" he said.

"Five," Richie declared confidently as Mattie, Wendy, and Charlotte stood by in anticipation.

"You sure you wanna take that bet?" Pearson asked as he squared himself toward a makeshift target on a rock by the river.

Richie looked toward the fading sunset, figuring that it would help his odds, smiled and replied, "Yep, five ripe ones."

"OK," Pearson said as he shook his legs and shoulders in preparation. Then he gazed with laser focus toward the target and spat the blackberry seed out, hitting the bullseye.

"No way! How did you do that? I can barely see a thing out here," Richie exclaimed as Mattie and Charlotte gasped. Wendy smiled and nodded her head, thoroughly impressed.

Pearson waved Richie over. As he came close, Pearson pointed at his eyes. "You see these? Two words for you: night vision." Then Pearson patted Richie on the head. "Looking forward to my tasty treats."

Richie playfully tackled Pearson and they began wrestling. Pearson couldn't get a handle on Richie because of his slick exterior. Richie teased him in return as he rubbed his arm. "You feel this? Two words for you: slippery skin."

Mattie, Charlotte, and Wendy laughed as they headed

back to where they had eaten dinner by the river. There were bats circling above, so Mattie grabbed a couple of empty clamshells from dinner and set them in front of her. She began banging a drumbeat on them loudly to scare the soaring creatures away. Any fear was quickly replaced by joy when Charlotte started wiggling and dancing to the rhythm. Charlotte loved it when Mattie played, and the feeling was mutual. Mattie couldn't stop smiling at Charlotte's free-spirited dancing. Wendy watched the entire spontaneous, beautiful cacophony of wrestling, drumming, and dancing along the riverbank. She smiled and said, "This is what it means to be wild and alive … life is as untamed and unruly as the river."

Later that night, while Mattie and Wendy lay next to each other under the stars, Mattie turned toward the mama otter. "I finally feel like I'm home. We've only been here a few months, but this is the first time in my life that I don't feel the need to perform, produce or prove myself. You all just love me for me."

A tear fell from Mattie's eye, which Wendy caught tenderly. "We don't give a fiddle about what you can or can't do. All we want is for you to enjoy life and connection with us."

Mattie placed her paw on Wendy's paw. "How odd that a naked porcupine feels more at home with otters and an albino animal than with her own kind."

Then Mattie giggled and said, "Speaking of which, do you have any guesses on what Pearson is?"

"A sharpshooter when it comes to blackberry spitting contests," Wendy replied. "Does it really matter what he is? In my book, what matters is that he has a good heart and he genuinely cares about you."

Mattie said, "That he does, with no strings attached."

"I'd say that's more than enough. Just enjoy Pearson's presence, without possessing or defining it … or *him* for that matter. After all, one creature's undivided attention and love are all it takes to heal the heart," Wendy said.

Mattie nodded, reflecting on the mama otter's wisdom. As she fell asleep listening to the bubbling river and the breeze rustling the leaves of a tree, Mattie thought of the grand, wise oak tree in the forest. It was just as he had advised—be still enough to discover that you are loved, not for what you can give and do, but for who you are. The river had taught her to relax and let go. All of nature was conspiring for her to come face to face with the hurt, scared little warrior inside herself, who just wanted to be loved.

27

THE ULTIMATE ALL-ACCESS PASS

ONE DAY, MATTIE FELT A STIRRING TO EXPLORE, SO SHE did as the tree advised and listened to her body. She wandered into a nearby forest that reminded her of her porcupine family. Mattie wondered what they might be up to. *Did Mom return to the family now that I'm not there?* She missed them dearly, despite their betrayal, and wanted to see them again, though she hesitated because they might be better off now without the anomaly in the family.

As she made her way back to their dwelling by the river, Pearson was wrestling with Richie. It was quickly becoming their favorite pastime, especially for Richie, given his clear advantage. Mattie smiled as Pearson huffed and puffed while continually trying to grab the slippery otter, however difficult that was.

Wendy and Charlotte set the strawberries and some newly smashed clams on the shore. The mama otter called, "Chow time!"

Pearson and Richie ran over and chomped down on the feast. Mattie was slow to eat, still thinking of her family. Wendy gently placed her paw on Mattie and asked, "You OK? You're barely touching your favorite treats."

"I love it here," said Mattie. "You've become family to me. But I can't help wondering what's going on back at home."

Wendy said, "I understand. That's how I felt when Daniel disappeared."

"Who's Daniel?" Mattie asked.

"The love of my life," replied Wendy.

"I miss Dad," chimed in Charlotte, softly.

"Me too, baby," said Wendy.

After a few moments of silent reflection, Wendy continued, "He suddenly disappeared. We didn't know where he was for months." Mattie gently put her paw on Wendy's.

"Finally, our neighbor, Roger, discovered that a hunter got to him down river," Wendy said with disgust. "That's why we don't go too far down the river anymore." She looked into Mattie's eyes. "We don't like to bring it up because it's too painful. Then you two showed up, and you helped fill the void that Daniel left. You brought such joy to us. And Pearson, he's brought Richie out of his shell, just like his dad used to."

Mattie gave Wendy a warm embrace. She thought, *Wow, we haven't been trying to do anything but be ourselves. I guess that's enough.*

Wendy continued, "You'll always be a part of our family, but they're your flesh and blood. They're a key piece of who you are."

"I really miss them," said Mattie.

Wendy thought for a few moments, then her face brightened up. "We can ask Roger. He knows everything."

"Everything?" Mattie said.

"Yes, he's a rat. Think about it, they go wherever they want, whenever they want—the ultimate all-access pass. Plus, they share all the latest gossip with each other. I'll go find him tomorrow morning."

Mattie hugged Wendy and said, "Thank you."

28

AWWW, RATS

Mattie was with Pearson by the river. She paced back and forth, anxious about what the rat might say. Frowning, she said to Pearson, "Who knows? They might all be dead already. Maybe I'm too late."

She began beating the ground shouting, "I never should've left!"

Pearson put his paw on her shoulder. "Yes, that's good. Get it all out." Noticing several leaves floating down the river. Pearson pointed to them and said, "You see those leaves?"

Mattie nodded.

"Those are like your emotions. It's important to acknowledge and name them, but if you cling to them and don't release them, they'll whisk you away," Pearson said.

She imagined herself gripping the leaves tightly and being carried by a roaring rapid into jagged rocks. Pearson put his paw on her head. "But if you just observe and allow them to flow through you, you'll stay right where you belong—here."

Turning to Pearson, whose eyes were filled with affection toward her, Mattie's breathing slowed and she was present again. She smiled and said, "How did you become such a wise sage?"

Pearson chuckled. "You see these triangular ears on the top of my head and my long muzzle?"

"Yeah?"

"Well, they're not for decoration."

Mattie chuckled. "Don't forget about your beady eyes, Mr. Observant."

"Well, I can't say it's all genetic. I've also made a few wise friends along the way," said Pearson, grinning at Mattie. He turned toward the river. A moment later, Wendy popped out of the water swimming upstream toward them.

"He's not far behind," Wendy said.

Pearson sniffed a bit and then dry hurled, "Yeah, I can smell him." Mattie giggled.

A nearby sage bush rustled a bit as a fat rat popped out, and said, "Smell who?"

The rat looked up at Mattie and Pearson and yelped.

"What the heck are you guys?" Roger asked with a puzzled look.

Wendy moved closer to Mattie and Pearson and whispered, "Sorry, he's a little blunt."

Mattie said, "Well, I'm Mattie, first of all." She put her paw out toward Roger for a handshake. He responded suspiciously by tapping it.

"And I'm Pearson." Pearson extended his paw.

Roger wouldn't shake it and asked, "Are you a predator?"

"Do I look like one?" Pearson said.

They stared at each other intensely. Roger examined Pearson's physique, then Mattie jumped in to defend Pearson.

"I've only seen him eat fruits and veggies. If he is a predator, he must be starving,"

Roger said, "Well, he does look on the skinnier side."

Wendy cackled awkwardly, creating an interruption. She

turned toward Roger. "Well, as I mentioned, we'd like your help in locating Mattie's family."

Mattie jumped in and said, "Yeah, do you know where the porcupines are?"

"You're a porcupine!?" Roger exclaimed.

Mattie was hurt and insulted by the tone of his response. She said, "Yeah, I am. Just because I don't have quills doesn't mean I'm not one."

Roger said, "No, that's not what I meant. The porcupines are about to get attacked by coyotes!"

Mattie became distraught. Pearson put his paw on her to comfort her but looked away guiltily.

"Are you sure?" Pearson asked.

Roger replied, "One hundred percent. My family and I are stocking up our burrow for when they come through. Rumor has it they have a charismatic new leader who is not even a coyote. He was able to convince the coyotes to attack the most elite porcupine clan in the land—which makes no sense if you ask me."

"That's my clan! Could we beat them if we left now?" Mattie asked without a moment of hesitation.

Roger gawked at Mattie, who appeared so defenseless. "You can't be serious. What are you going to do, lecture them as they devour you?"

Mattie ignored his snide remark and asked, "What's the fastest route?"

Wendy turned toward Mattie and chimed in, "You sure you want to do this? He's got a point."

"I don't care what happens to me. I need to at least try to protect them," Mattie said.

Pearson turned to Roger and asked, "So, which way's the fastest?"

"Well, you can't say I didn't warn ya," Roger said. "You can follow the river, which will take about a week."

Mattie shook her head. "That's too long. Are there any other options?"

"OK, swashbuckler. Well, I haven't been there in years, but there's Curtains Cave," Roger replied.

Wendy gasped, "Curtains Cave?"

She put her paw on Mattie. "I don't think that's a good idea. It's best if you go by river. Plus, I can join you."

"How much faster is Curtains Cave?" asked Mattie without skipping a beat.

Roger rubbed his brow and said, "It'll take you about half the time. That's if you make it out alive. We don't call it Curtains Cave for nothing." He made a slitting motion on his neck to emphasize his point and with a mobster accent, added, "It's curtains for ya!"

"I don't care what they call it. Which way do we go?" Mattie asked as she let out a little squeak. Her legs were trembling, giving her away.

Roger shook his head and pointed toward the ominous, saw-toothed hills far in the western horizon. "Head toward the peak of the tallest hill. You'll find a small opening the size of two mountain lions."

As Mattie surveyed the distant hillside, she realized she was seeing the backside of the valley she grew up in. But she had never been through the cave because her mom had warned her that it was too dangerous.

"Wait, do lions live in that cave?" said Wendy.

Roger shrugged his shoulders. "Maybe. I've only scurried through there once, and I told myself I'd never do it again."

Pearson shook his head. Roger looked annoyed then motioned to Mattie to come close and whispered in her ear, "My two cents, take it or leave it. Don't go with the albino. There's something off about him."

Agitated, Mattie said, "I'm not leaving without him. He's my friend." She emphasized her point by standing right beside Pearson in a show of support for him.

PART IV:

HOMECOMING

29

(PULL BACK) THE CURTAINS CAVE

MATTIE AND PEARSON'S LAST SUPPER WITH THE OTTERS was bittersweet. Mattie had finally found a sense of belonging and now she had to say goodbye. Tears welled up in her eyes. Wendy and Charlotte snuggled close to her. Wendy said, "You're like a daughter to me. You are welcome back anytime. We'll always be home to you."

She pulled out a makeshift necklace made of twine with a clamshell as the pendant.

"This is to remind you of the river's lesson, that day we cracked you open like a clam," Wendy said and put it around Mattie's neck.

Charlotte nuzzled herself into Mattie's arms. "You're still the most beautiful creature I've ever seen, with or without flowers."

As Charlotte's words sank deep into Mattie's heart, tears rolled down her cheeks.

Pearson looked on with affection when Richie tackled him out of nowhere. They all laughed as Pearson and Richie had one last tussle, rolling and tumbling along the shore as they were accustomed to doing. Richie wasn't comfortable with emotional goodbyes. This was how he let Pearson know how much he loved him—getting close and intimate in the form of wrestling.

On their difficult ascent, right before a corner where they could no longer see the river, Mattie and Pearson looked back for one final glimpse of what had become their home. They were surprised to see their beloved otter family still watching as they made their way up the rocky ridge. They waved their paws and saw the otters off in the distance wave back. Turning the corner, they saw the small opening that Roger had described.

Chills went up and down Mattie's spine as she let out a quiet squeak. The closer they got, the more she wanted to go back to the comfortable, familiar river. She began doubting herself. Thoughts raced through her head. *Am I on a suicide mission? Maybe we're already too late. This is dumb. Why am I jeopardizing my life for a clan that exiled me?*

She hardly noticed arriving at the cave's entrance. Seeing her anguish, Pearson put his paw on her shoulder.

"Remember the leaves in the river?"

It freaked her out how well Pearson knew her, but it also made sense since she had never been good at hiding her emotions. She was a naked porcupine who wore her heart on her sleeve. Mattie paused at the cave's opening, staring into the abyss. She shivered at the thought of what might be awaiting them in the cave. Mountain lions? Snakes? No exit on the other side? Unending darkness?

One thing she knew for sure awaited her—the unknown, and this scared her more than anything else. As she stood shaking to her core, Pearson looked into her eyes. "You don't have to do this."

Mattie shook her head. "Yes, I do."

And before her mind could get the better of her, she

stepped into the darkness. With each step, there was less visibility. About twenty-five steps in, it became pitch black. At that moment, she was particularly aware of both the blessing and the curse of being naked. She was highly sensitive to the heat coming off Pearson's body to reassure her she wasn't completely alone. But if there happened to be a predator in the cave, she had no quills to protect herself. She only had her trust in Pearson to defend her.

As she thought about Pearson, Roger's warning echoed in her head, "There's something off about him." Fear gripped her again as she thought of this being the perfect moment for Pearson to attack her. No witnesses, no evidence. After all, everyone but the otters had betrayed her—Christian, George, Sirk the ringmaster, and most of all, her own flesh and blood that she was risking her life for in this terrifying cave.

Anger and grief boiled in her veins as she stewed about the injustice she had experienced her entire life. *And for what reason? Something she couldn't control—being born a spineless porcupine.* She quivered with rage and self-hatred. All she ever wanted was to be someone different than who she was. She couldn't hold it in anymore and roared at the top of her lungs, "Why was I born this way?!"

Her words echoed in the vastness of the cave, revealing its depths as the sound waves bounced around its dark corridors. An eerie silence followed her abrupt but long overdue outburst. Somehow in the darkness, she felt free enough to lose all composure and bare her soul. Not only was her body naked, but now her soul as well. In this liminal space of feeling on the edge of death where darkness seemed to have no end, she could let the dam break on her loss and grief that she had been suppressing with busyness.

She broke down and collapsed into a ball, cradling herself on the cold dark ground. Pearson came close, but she pushed him away. She wanted to be alone because that was how she felt inside—abandoned, misunderstood, empty, and in the dark about so much. *Though she tried so hard to do the right thing, why was she continuously met with betrayal, pain, and rejection? Where was the justice in that?*

Suddenly a calm, quiet, motherly voice from above broke the silence, "If I answer why, would I be answering your head or your heart?"

Though Mattie had every reason to be frightened by this strange, unexpected voice, she felt its presence and it was warm, reassuring, and full of peace.

"You'd be answering me," Mattie said.

"But if you knew why, would that satisfy your head or your heart?" the voice said. "Your head asks the 'why' questions, but your heart asks the 'where' and 'how' questions. 'Where are the ones who will love me as I am? How am I lovable just as I am? How is the way I was born a good thing?' Those are the answers that will satisfy your heart. Do you want to know the answer to those questions?"

Mattie answered faintly, "Yes."

Another voice similar to the first one but masculine said, "We've been watching you, Mattie. Think back on your journey so far. Where were the ones who loved you as you were? Pearson, the tree, the otters. Don't they all have flaws and tragedies like yours that they have learned to embrace?"

She reflected on the magnificent iridescent sunset through the battered branches of the towering tree. She also thought of Pearson, her mysterious albino animal friend who was abused and rejected by the circus, and the otters who suffered the tremendous loss of their beloved Daniel.

"Yes," Mattie replied.

"Would they be the compassionate beings they are today without the heart-wrenching journey they've gone through?" asked the male voice.

Mattie thought about it and realized that what the tree, Pearson, and the otters had in common was that they all decided to turn their pain into compassion instead of drowning in the waters of bitterness. She said aloud, "No, their tears formed deep crevices in their hearts, and they chose to transform them into reservoirs of love."

"Yes, it is a choice to enter into the alchemy of transforming pain into empathy. And that involves us choosing not to avoid or numb our wounds but tending to them with the utmost kindness," the female voice said.

The fatherly voice above them continued, "So the ones who unconditionally love you are the ones who are wounded, yet aware and humble enough to embrace it in themselves and others."

The female voice said, "The paradox for you to understand is that you aren't broken or loved, messy or beautiful. You are broken and loved, messy and beautiful."

Mattie asked, "Who are you?"

She heard wings begin flapping above, then squeaking around her. She knew they were bats, whom she had always hated. But this didn't make sense. Like most animals, she was taught to fear bats and here they were, so full of wisdom and compassion. She didn't realize how much bias she had until it was dark enough to see the truth of their hearts, as well as her own.

The male voice interrupted her thoughts. "Who taught us how to fly?"

Mattie said, "I don't know. It came naturally to you?"

"We've seen you build traps and perform circus tricks. But you learned how to do those things for approval. But what comes naturally to you?" he said.

After thinking for a while, Mattie replied. "Feeling. I can feel exactly where you are above me. I can feel every autumn breeze and know there will be a changing of the seasons. I can feel the heat of the ground when summer is upon us. I can sense every subtle movement like you just know how to fly."

The female bat said, "So let your gift of sensitivity define you, not what you've learned or suffered in order to be accepted. Being spineless is your superpower, not your weakness."

Mattie said, "But feeling everything sucks! Do you know how much it hurts when I'm rejected and betrayed?"

The female bat replied, "Yes. The only reason others hurt you is because they were first wounded themselves. Hurt beings hurt beings. It's not because they're evil or bad. It also doesn't mean you need to fix or trust them either. We've seen you use your keen sensitivity and intuition to quickly learn survival skills to cope with that pain. You've brilliantly controlled and avoided potentially volatile circumstances based on your instinct to no longer be rejected and hurt. But this protection has shielded you from good things as well."

"Like?" Mattie asked.

"Us," the male bat said.

"Sometimes we need to keep some good out to avoid the bad," Mattie said.

"We were there all along to help you, but you feared us. We tried to get your attention, but you were so fixated on protecting and proving yourself," the wise male bat said.

"But I want to prove my family wrong! That I am someone they should be proud of, not ashamed of!" Mattie blurted out with much more anger than she had intended.

Pearson finally said, "But you're missing all the good around you while you're preoccupied with your need for justice, Mattie."

"We see everything, especially in the night when no one thinks they're being watched," the motherly bat said as she landed in front of Mattie. "The truth always comes out. It cannot stay hidden. The seeds we sow will inevitably show what we did with our lives, especially when we thought no one was watching."

The male bat added, "We've been watching you, Mattie.

You have a good heart. We've seen the good seed you've sown and that you are always trying to do good for others. You might not see the fruit in your lifetime. But keep doing good. It's who you are. The fruit will come."

Mattie let out a huge sigh. She didn't realize she was holding her breath for a specific idea of justice, mainly one where both her porcupine clan and circus family apologized and embraced her as their own. Mattie truly did miss out on so much good by being fixated on her idea of justice with them. It was as if a heavy burlap cloth had been taken off of her, and she could enjoy the sunshine of those who loved her just as she was—a naked, sensitive porcupine.

Ironically, this enlightenment was happening in a pitch-black cave, but life had never seemed brighter. She could finally be herself, with nothing to prove. After all, if she wasn't a spineless porcupine, Mattie wouldn't be able to do what she really wanted to do next—cuddle with the bats whose names she didn't know but were now family to her, just like the other animals she had come to know. And that was exactly what she did. They were so warm and fuzzy with their velvety wings, nothing like she imagined but precisely what she needed at that moment.

After a while, Mattie found it awkward being so intimate with these bats when she didn't even know their names. While she was nuzzled by one of the bats, she said, "By the way, I'm Madeline. Also known as the sensitive porcupine."

The female bat chuckled. "I know, Mattie. I'm Michelle."

"And I'm Jack. It's nice to officially meet you," the male bat chimed in.

Michelle said, "From the moment you and your mom wandered into our cave many years ago, we've been watching over you."

Mattie looked around and realized it was the very cave

her mom had hidden her in to protect her from a roaming bobcat when she was little.

"You were so tiny and vulnerable, our hearts couldn't help but melt, especially after Jasmine attacked you with her spines. We decided we would do everything we could to help you," Jack said.

Michelle giggled, adding, "Which wasn't easy, of course, because you couldn't stand the sight of us!"

Mattie laughed as she remembered all the times she had shooed the bats away without a thought of talking to them.

Pearson, who was close by, joined the cuddle fest. "Yes, sometimes the ones we're most afraid of are the very ones who have the most to offer us."

30

HOMECOMING

Using their echolocation, Jack and Michelle guided Mattie and Pearson out of the pitch-black cave. When they emerged, Mattie was astonished to see the beautiful valley where she grew up. She could see the forest, lusher and more mature than she remembered. She was flooded with memories of hiding traps with Mikey and Jasmine, wearing the bell around her neck at warrior school, and the trial that led to her being banished from the clan. So much had changed inside of her, yet it all felt so familiar like it had happened yesterday.

Mattie began doubting herself and said, "I don't know if I can do this."

Pearson leaned into her. "You're right. *You* can't do this." Then he looked over at Jack and Michelle and continued, "But *we* can … together."

Mattie nodded and smiled when she realized this was not like the past. As Michelle and Jack stood on either side of her, she remembered she was never alone. Pearson scanned the horizon with his laser-sharp vision and pointed toward the grassy landscape west of the forest. "The coyotes are over there!"

The band was making their way quietly toward the porcupine clan. Pearson turned toward Mattie and shouted, "Hop on!" She quickly jumped on Pearson's back, and they took off while Michelle and Jack flew above them. All of Mattie's training in the circus maintaining her balance on Nelson the elephant really paid off.

The coyotes were perplexed when the foursome descended toward them, as they saw a naked porcupine riding an albino animal with two wily bats soaring above in tow. As they got closer, Mattie was shocked to see that a monkey donning a red vest was leading the coyotes toward the porcupines. She squinted and gasped as she pondered aloud, "Christian?"

Pearson asked, "What? Where?"

Mattie tapped Pearson's left shoulder to indicate the direction where he was. "Over there. He's their new leader!"

This made perfect sense. Christian was quite charismatic and convincing when it came to cajoling animals into his schemes. Though Mattie wondered how and why he had left his beloved circus. Christian was just as surprised when he saw Pearson and Mattie barreling toward him with two bats. He barked out a command to the coyotes next to him, "Stop them!"

The coyotes charged toward Pearson and Mattie but getting close, they slowed down in disbelief. The nearest coyote asked, "Is that you, Pearson?"

Pearson slowed down, nodded, and whispered, "Hannah, I hoped I'd see you again."

Hannah looked at Pearson affectionately. Mattie observed their strong connection and wracked her brain. *Why does that name sound so familiar?*

Mattie saw that Pearson was overcome with emotion as if he were reuniting with an old flame. His heart beat so wildly that it even rocked Mattie with its rhythm. Pearson tenderly nuzzled nose to nose with Hannah as she blushed.

Mattie's eyes widened while she watched because it looked as if they were kissing. She squirmed at such a wild and uncomfortable turn of events. "Umm, awkward," slipped through her lips.

Then a male coyote growled and wedged himself between Hannah and Pearson as the other coyotes encircled them and sniffed at Pearson. Mattie was horrified to be a foot away from her mortal enemies, with only her dear albino friend keeping her from becoming their next meal. The male coyote who had interrupted Hannah and Pearson growled at Mattie.

Pearson yapped, "No, David! She's my friend."

Christian arrived. "What are you waiting for?"

"He's one of us," David said.

"So?!" Christian roared.

"We don't attack our own," Hannah said, as the band around Mattie and Pearson became calm.

"You're a coyote?!" Mattie yelled at Pearson, jumping off him.

The other coyotes swiftly approached Mattie, licking their lips. She yelped, as Jack and Michelle had landed next to her to block them. Mattie hastily tapped Pearson's leg to lower for her to hop on, which he promptly did. She jumped back on.

Mattie whispered into his ear, "Why didn't you tell me?"

"Would you have trusted me?" Pearson asked.

Mattie confessed, "No."

"Exactly," said Pearson.

Christian walked up to Mattie. "I should've known I would run into you eventually."

Baffled, Mattie asked, "Why did you leave the circus?"

Christian snickered bitterly. "Leave?! Sirk traced *your* tar back to me and banished me. He left me with nothing. No food, water, shelter, family. Nothing."

Christian was close to Mattie and glared at her with rage and spat, "And it was all your fault!"

Mattie shook her head, confused. "How was it my fault?"

"Before you came to the circus, everything was great. I had a family, a home—everyone adored me. You took all that away from me!" Christian snickered spitefully. "Thankfully, I was able to befriend this lovely band who were also famished," as he looked at the coyotes surrounding them.

Pearson turned toward the coyotes asking, "Why didn't you just eat him?"

Christian padded his body and said, "I'm but skin and bones. So, I offered my services of climbing high into trees and spying the land for defenseless food sources instead."

"He was able to locate a colony of delicious rabbits for us. It's hard to argue with that, especially since there's been less and less prey over the years," said David.

Hannah turned to Pearson, "We've had to roam further to find adequate food."

"There is another way. Berries are just as delicious," said Pearson as he shook his head, thinking of all the potential friends that were lost due to their ignorant consumption of other animals.

Christian interrupted and scoffed, "But not as yummy as decrepit porcupines." The conniving monkey winked at the coyotes. "Am I right?"

Pearson said, "So you convinced them to attack Mattie's clan?"

"A family for a family, right? Wouldn't you say that's justice?" Christian said.

"No, because it'll never satisfy the void in your heart," said Mattie.

"How do you know?"

"Because vengeance only balances the scales in your

mind, not your heart," Mattie said, reflecting on her conversation with Jack and Michelle in the cave.

David turned toward Christian angrily and sputtered, "Wait, you never told us this was about revenge."

"You said that these porcupines were easy prey," another coyote growled as he circled Christian.

"Are you kidding me? We're the best-trained porcupines in the land. We go to a warrior school for years and only the best graduate!" said Mattie proudly.

Mattie's heart filled with gratitude toward her father who had pushed so hard to make the warrior school an elite one. His heart was good, though misguided at times. He only wanted to protect the clan from ever having another tragedy like his father's.

Enraged, the coyotes surrounded Christian, ready to attack as he screamed, "Wait, she's lying! I saw them with my own eyes! They're mostly old, weak, and disoriented. She's just trying to protect her helpless clan."

Mattie spoke to the coyotes, "Have you heard of Spencer, the porcupine commander?"

"Yeah, I thought he was just a legend," David said.

Mattie held her chest up high, "No, that's my dad! And my clan is just as menacing as they are in the stories. Christian was leading you into a bloodbath with them."

"You never told me your dad was Spencer?" said Pearson with surprise.

Jack flapped his wings for emphasis, "It's true. And Mattie is an heir. She could very well become the next commander." Michelle nodded.

Pearson arched his head to look at Mattie and smiled, "I guess we're all learning things about each other, aren't we?"

Mattie murmured, "Well, it would've been true had I been born with spines."

"It's a courageous heart that makes a commander, not their quills," said Jack.

"And you definitely have a courageous heart, Madeline," Michelle said.

The coyotes were ready to pounce on Christian but Mattie yelled at them, "Wait!"

Mattie's motioned for Jack and Michelle to come close and whispered to them, "Would you be able to find out where Christian's parents are?"

Jack and Michelle looked at each other, and Michelle said, "That's if they're still alive."

"Give us a couple days," Jack said confidently.

Turning to the coyotes, Mattie said, "Since this was an attack against my clan, let Pearson and I decide what punishment Christian should suffer."

Pearson reassured his band, "We'll make sure justice is served."

The coyotes agreed because even though they rejected Pearson for being an albino, he had never sought vengeance and had always proved himself to be respectful and trustworthy. Christian let out a sigh while still fearing for his life. Mattie whispered to Jack and Michelle, "They're probably still performing in a nearby circus."

Michelle nodded, then gave Mattie a quick snuggle before Jack and her soared off in search of Christian's parents.

Before the coyotes left, Hannah said to Pearson, "I'm sorry for how I hurt you. It took you leaving for me to realize what I had lost. What we all had lost. Will you return to us?"

David watched Pearson and Hannah suspiciously and began pacing over. Pearson leaned toward her and murmured, "Are you happy?"

"David is good to me, but I do miss you," said Hannah.

Briefly, Pearson looked sad but seeing Mattie, he said to Hannah, "I've missed you, too. But I've found my family.

Please take care of yourself and have those pups you've always dreamed of."

David approached with an envious glare. Mattie got defensive of Pearson and even though it meant facing off with a dreaded coyote, she headed over as well to be between David and Pearson. Pearson watched Mattie as she puffed up her body and marched over as intimidatingly and defiantly as she possibly could. Pearson chuckled and shook his head, waving for her to stay where she was. Mattie grumbled but stopped.

Pearson reassured David, "Please take good care of her, she's a special one," as he bowed to signal that he would no longer pursue Hannah. David eased and nodded with respect. They all touched noses before the band of coyotes headed toward the horizon.

Mattie finished her strut over to Pearson and wondered aloud, "What was that all about?"

Pearson smiled. "Some much-needed closure."

Mattie leaned into Pearson and said, "Don't worry, you're still my favorite coyote."

Pearson grinned, and Mattie continued, "And no, I will never get used to saying that!"

31

THE DIAMOND UNDER
THE DISGUISE

MATTIE HANDED CHRISTIAN A BLACKBERRY SHE plucked from the bush they were resting under. He looked suspiciously at it and sniffed it.

"Are you trying to poison me?"

Mattie laughed. "If you don't want it, hand it over."

Pearson sat next to Christian, keeping him under close watch to make sure he didn't escape or worse, harm Mattie. Christian licked the berry, then gobbled it down in one bite. After it cleared his throat, he said, "I think the tar gave you brain damage. You're dumb to spare me. Trust me, I'll eventually outwit you and find a way to destroy you and your clan."

Mattie rubbed her forehead, astonished that Christian was so brilliant yet so twisted in how he interpreted the world. Trauma blinds you in that way, she realized as she thought about how being bullied when she was a young porcupette had caused her initially to lash out at the kindness and wisdom of the owls. She said, "I know you meant to harm me, but you tarring me was one of the best things that happened to me."

Christian looked perplexed. Mattie could see he couldn't

understand why someone was being kind to him when all he wanted to do was harm them. It caused him to feel out of control. Anticipating and provoking familiar behavior would make him feel safe because then he would understand what they were doing, and thus be more adept at preventing himself from being hurt again. Mattie knew that he would try to regain control of the situation by doing everything in his power to incite her to behave in a way he could predict, such as arguing with him. He jeered, "Yep, you have brain damage," snapped Christian.

Mattie chuckled as she shook her head, much to his dismay. "I had to depend on Pearson, which I would never have done otherwise. Also, you forced me out of a world that was too small for me. One I would've never let go of even though it was suffocating me."

Christian scoffed at the idea of anywhere being better than the circus. He rolled his eyes mockingly. "You're just making up excuses for why you're a loser who can't perform anymore." Pearson growled angrily in his face, making Christian sit attentively like a good schoolboy and listen.

Mattie came closer to Christian. "I also realized that if we don't heal from our wounds, we recreate them. Until we're brave enough to trust others and take off our masks, we will continue in the lonely cycle of being admired from a distance yet terrified of ever truly being known. We'll keep wrapping ourselves in all that glitters, not knowing the truth —that we are a diamond concealing something far more beautiful than our disguise."

She put her paw on Christian's shoulder. "I honestly don't think we're that different. We were both abandoned by our families at a young age, and from that moment on, we've been trying to prove ourselves back into belonging. Yet, no matter how hard we try, the very ones we want to please the most leave us. That's because we abandoned ourselves first. Our disguises told them that we were only as good as our last trick. A wise friend once told me, 'It isn't love if you have to perform for it. It isn't acceptance if you have to pretend for it.'"

Mattie nodded at Pearson in acknowledgment, who blushed.

She looked into Christian's eyes and smiled sincerely, "And that's what I learned since leaving the circus. So, if anything, I should thank you."

Christian was looking utterly baffled and, caught off guard, he blurted out, "Seriously, what the heck happened to you?"

She reflected on her wild adventure for a moment and said, "Well, a battered tree taught me to slow down and rest, and that life is not a zero-sum game with a limited amount of success to go around—we can all succeed together. A group of facetious owls taught me to not take myself so seriously. Then, some precious otters taught me what it means to belong to a family. A river taught me to relax and enjoy the ride. But most of all, an albino coyote and a couple of bats taught me that who we fear most are often the very ones who hold the key to our freedom."

"And what key is that?" Christian asked.

Mattie pondered for a moment, then said, "I used to believe that if I did everything perfectly, I would find fulfillment in life. I now realize that allowing myself to be loved, mess and all is the only way I will ever find fulfillment in life."

"Is that it?" Christian said.

Mattie and Pearson chuckled. Mattie couldn't help herself. She hugged Christian. "I missed you!"

He stiffened in her embrace and awkwardly pushed her away, "OK, that's enough." Mattie whispered softly into Christian's ear before she let go, "I know you only exclude others because you don't feel included. But soon enough, you'll know that you belong."

32

THE PERFECT MATCH

MATTIE WAS FAST ASLEEP WHILE CHRISTIAN LAY WIDE awake mulling over Mattie's words. That was when Jack and Michelle abruptly landed right in front of them in the still dark of night, startling them. Mattie screamed as she awoke, "Who's there?"

Christian yelped as he shot up and stumbled over himself, "Mommy!"

Pearson, nearby keeping watch, was amused by how disoriented Mattie and Christian were.

"Mattie, we found them!" Michelle announced with glee, flapping her wings excitedly.

Christian rubbed his eyes and asked, "Found who?"

"Well, it's funny you yelled 'mommy' because that's exactly who they found along with your daddy," Mattie said, shaking off her grogginess.

"That's impossible. I doubt they're even still alive." Christian said with disbelief. "Nice try. I'm not falling for one of your tricks to get rid of me."

"Why would I want to get rid of you?" Mattie asked, genuinely perplexed. "Why is it so hard for you to believe that my intentions are good toward you?"

Christian said, "Because I wasn't born yesterday. Everyone's looking out for themselves, including you."

Mattie shook her head. Then Michelle opened up one of her wings to reveal that she was holding a little red toy drumstick. She handed it to Christian. "I believe this belongs to you."

As soon as it touched Christian's hand, tears formed in his eyes. From inside his vest pocket, he pulled out the beat-up little toy drumstick he carried and put them together side by side. They matched perfectly. Tears began streaming down Christian's cheeks. Mattie wrapped herself around him and Pearson soon followed. Jack and Michelle spread their wings over all of them, like a cocoon.

Christian's weeping was like a river washing over the desert lands of his heart causing his innocence to blossom again like wild poppies after a long drought. Mattie thought, *Could he feel the little baby monkey within him awakening —the one he had been before being abandoned, the one who believed that anything was possible? The one who believed that the world was ultimately good. After all, the greatest longing he buried deep within his heart was about to be fulfilled—being reunited with his mom and dad.*

He whispered softly, "They're alive?"

Jack said, "Yes, they're so thrilled at being reunited with you again."

"How did you find them?" Christian said.

Michelle giggled, boasting, "If you think rats know everything, just imagine if they had wings."

Christian laughed and smiled. He put his hand on Michelle's shoulder and conveyed with sincerity, "Thank you."

Michelle looked into his eyes. "You're welcome. But you really should thank Mattie, it was her idea." Christian looked over at Mattie who gave him a sweet but sheepish smile.

Christian wrapped his arms around Mattie. "OK, fine. You win. You have a good heart."

"And so do you," Mattie replied as she embraced him in return.

33

STRAWBERRY FIELDS FOREVER

Pearson roamed their surroundings and scrounged up a few strawberries for their farewell meal with Christian. The delectable fruit had been Mattie and Christian's favorite treat at the circus when they performed well. No tricks were being done here though, just hearts blossoming in the warmth of each other's presence after a long, cold winter of bitterness.

The group savored every bite as well as their precious time together. Christian became antsy with regret and shared vulnerably with Mattie, "I wish I hadn't spent so much time hating you."

"It's not your fault, Christian," Mattie replied tenderly. "You were only recreating what had first been done to you."

Christian's face was still downcast, so she put her paw on his back. "You can forgive yourself." He nodded as a tear rolled down his cheek. After a few moments of silence, the monkey turned toward Mattie and said, "I'll miss you, dear friend."

The sun set like a fleeting rainbow set aflame in a bed of sapphire. Nature seemed to know it was a poignant moment —Christian breaking the cycle of suffering with forgiveness

—and punctuated it with its beauty. He pulled out the drumsticks from his red vest. Christian began beating slowly on the ground. As he played, the rhythm pacified his wounds and regulated his heartbeat. The tempo fluctuated then began to pick up—it was following the frequency of both grief for what was lost yet also celebration for what was now set into motion, a cycle of healing.

They all began swaying and dancing to Christian's rhythm and for the first time, his drumming wasn't for a master or an audience. It was for those who heard it to come into sync with the natural beating of their own hearts.

After a while, the rhythm slowed and faded along with the dimming sun. Michelle and Jack stretched out their wings, ready to take Christian to his parents. Christian handed the drumsticks to Mattie. "Even though I taught you how to play, you're better than me. That's originally why I wanted to get rid of you. You surpassed me in what I had built my identity on."

Mattie shook her head and gave them back to him. "Better or worse is irrelevant. These belong to you."

"I don't need to perform anymore," Christian said.

Mattie asked, "But does it bring you joy?"

Christian grinned like an eager baby monkey.

"Then drum your heart out. But this time for yourself," Mattie said.

Christian grabbed the drumsticks and pumped his fists with them. He rocked out on his imaginary air drums with glee. Pearson, Mattie, and the bats laughed.

Giving Christian a final hug, Pearson and Mattie watched him beating the ground with his drumsticks and following the bats into the sunset. He turned back to yell at Mattie, "Until we meet again," and waved farewell. Mattie had no doubt that, as Christian played on their way to his parents, any creature hearing it would be awakened somehow to the longing in their hearts.

34

UNITY IS OUR GREATEST POWER

IT WAS TIME FOR MATTIE TO HAVE HER OWN REUNION. She was simultaneously thrilled and horrified about seeing her family again. *How will they respond? What will they think of me? Have they forgotten about me? Are they even still alive?*

Pearson could see what Mattie was going through. "I'll come with you."

"No, they'll attack you on sight," Mattie said.

"Fine, I'll go with you as far as I can, then hide and keep an eye on you. We have the cover of night on our side," said Pearson.

Mattie nodded her head, comforted to know that no matter what happened, Pearson would be right there watching over her, ready to support her in any way she needed.

Halfway through their journey back to her clan, her suspicions toward Pearson returned. After all, he was the mortal enemy she was taught to fear and despise all her life. All that training couldn't be wrong, could it? Aloud she asked, "Are you going to eat me? I mean, you are a coyote after all."

Pearson responded, "And coyotes eat berries and other

yummy things, not just porcupines. Though if your family are jerks, I might reconsider."

She grinned, saying, "Start with my dad and Trevor. They'll make a delectable meal."

"I'll have my fingers crossed," Pearson joked as he licked his lips. His humor always disarmed her and set her at ease.

As they drew near to the edge of the clan, Pearson hid in a lush, juniper tree where he had a bird's-eye view of the porcupines.

Pearson whispered to Mattie, "No matter what happens, you already belong. There's nothing to prove, 'k?" She nodded and gave him a nuzzle, then went toward the valley where the porcupines were gathered.

As Mattie crossed the ridge, Jasmine was the first to see her and squealed in delight. Jasmine hopped toward her, followed by two adorable little porcupettes whose quills hadn't hardened yet.

"You're home!" Jasmine shouted.

Mattie was bewildered. *When was this ever home?*

Jasmine then turned to her little ones. "Katie and Darius, this is your Auntie Mattie!"

Darius stared at Mattie and said, "What the heck? You're a porcupine?"

Katie, who was also staring with her mouth agape, eventually said under her breath, "You're related to us?"

Mattie smirked, amused by how cute yet prejudiced they were already. It made sense, though, since their grandfather was around to train them.

"And why do you have something around your neck?" Katie asked, pointing at the clam-shell necklace Wendy had made.

Mattie appreciated the timely reminder of her otter family when she was feeling so distant from her blood family.

Jasmine asked, "What happened to the bell?"

"You did," Mattie said through her teeth, not realizing she still had unresolved anger about the betrayal.

Jasmine looked ashamed and turned away, pretending not to hear what her sister had said. Then, toward the family den (where Mattie was born), Jasmine squealed, "Mattie's back." Pain welled in Mattie's heart to see the place where she had always wanted to belong but never could.

First, Jasmine's partner came out, awkwardly swatting away a spider's web blocking the entrance. Mattie chuckled, wondering if it might be the work of her long-lost friend, Mikey. She scanned the area but saw no sign of him.

The approaching male porcupine was rugged and tough. It made sense to Mattie that Jasmine would marry someone like their father. Just like Mattie, Jasmine tried desperately to gain the approval of their commander and dad. Approval, which was always dangled just out of reach, like the proverbial carrot on a stick. "This is Chris," Jasmine said, as her partner looked Mattie up and down like she was an alien.

Chris turned toward Jasmine. "What in the world?"

Jasmine growled under her breath, "You're being rude, just like your son. This is Mattie, the one I told you about."

Chris continued to stare at Mattie. Mattie grinned at him awkwardly.

Then their brother, Trevor, came out of the den, followed by his partner and two brawny male porcupettes who were bumping into each other, ready to start a fight. They were too busy to notice their spineless aunt.

"Like father, like sons," Mattie said, shaking her head. *Just what we need, more aggressive, oblivious porcupines in the world.*

Trevor's partner came over. "It's great to finally meet you. I'm Jeanne, and these two rambunctious ones are Colin and Paul."

When they heard their mom say their names, they

stopped fighting long enough to notice their aunt and froze at the sight of her.

Colin was the first to speak saying, "How can you be our aunt? You're not a porcupine."

"Yeah, porcupines have spines," Paul chimed in.

Mattie smiled at their feigned ignorance and said, "Well, isn't it your lucky day? You're getting to meet a spineless porcupine for the first time. There's more to being a porcupine than our defenses."

Trevor took a long hard look at Mattie and then mockingly said, "You still don't have quills?"

Mattie spoke before she could catch herself, "And you still don't have any tact?"

Trevor's two sons, Colin and Paul, giggled—which Mattie could see infuriated their insecure, controlling father. Trevor charged toward Mattie, but they all froze when they heard Josephine's voice echoing from within the den, "Is that you, Mattie?"

Mattie's mother limped out of the den slowly. All that time in exile must have worn down on her. Tears welled up in Mattie's eyes as she went as close as she could to her mom without getting pricked. She gazed longingly into her mom's eyes. "I've missed you so much."

Josephine gently placed her paw on Mattie's, careful not to let her quills touch her naked daughter, and smiled with contentment. Mattie's dad, Spencer, came out of the den last —not surprising, given his eagerness to hide Mattie's existence since the day she was born.

He was also much older and slower than she remembered. His shoulders were slumped, maybe from all those years of carrying the weight of his pride and responsibilities. All he could muster was a nod of acknowledgment toward his banished daughter. Mattie was grateful. It was one of the kindest gestures he'd ever given her. Josephine turned toward

Jasmine and Trevor. "Can you gather some bark? We need to celebrate Mattie's return."

During the meal, Mattie shared with them about becoming the headliner in the circus and how she had often imagined her family in the audience when she performed the most daring tricks. She shared about her befriending the tree, the owls, the otters, and the bats. Jasmine, Katie, Darius, and Josephine were intrigued and hung to her every word.

Katie shouted with excitement, "I want to go on a wilderness adventure like Auntie Mattie! It sounds so cool!"

"Yeah, I wanna play soccer with the owls!" Darius chimed in.

Jasmine, perhaps feeling a tinge of jealousy, quickly dismissed her porcupettes, "Don't be ridiculous. We are the envy of every porcupine because our clan occupies the best land for miles around."

"And how would you know that if you've never left this valley?" Mattie asked.

Jasmine glared at her looking like she wanted the conversation to be over. She growled, "Darius, Katie, eat faster now!"

All the while, Spencer was too distracted by Trevor and his boys, who quickly gobbled down the bark and began wrestling.

"They're such strong and healthy porcupettes," Spencer said proudly.

Trevor puffed up his chest and said, "Gotta live up to the name of commander, right?"

Mattie shook her head in disappointment. *How could they all be so narrow-minded and ignorant?* She realized that it was due to them never leaving their small, homogenous clan.

Wisdom would always be in short supply as long as they refused to interact with other creatures. Darius and Katie's curiosity gave her hope though. Maybe the next generation might learn that being different is a gift and be drawn to explore the vast wilderness. At least she may have planted the seeds of what was possible through her epic tales.

Josephine spoke up, "Well, now that Mattie's back and has a broad understanding of the land, I think she would make a wonderful commander."

Spencer stared at her in disbelief as she had both spoken up and challenged his authority. He said, "Don't be ridiculous. Trevor, Colin, and Paul are all more than capable of carrying on the legacy." Spencer pointed at the aggressive porcupettes. "Why, they're exactly how I was when I became commander. They'll keep our clan safe just like I have."

Mattie thought about how she and Pearson averted a coyote attack through their wits and diplomacy. She said, "Aggression isn't the only way to protect a clan."

Trevor jeered at Mattie, saying, "It's sheer luck you haven't been eaten yet. Let's see how long you can make it without us, you spineless coward!"

Mattie snapped back, "I have a *way* stronger backbone than you will ever have! I've been in the wilderness for years without any of you, which is a far more dangerous place than hiding in a clan full of spines. Luck or quills didn't keep me safe. Other animals did. Isn't that how our clan was formed? Understanding that unity is our greatest power?"

"Unity with our own kind!" Trevor barked. "If you feel *so* safe around other creatures, why don't you go back to them because you don't belong here."

Mattie answered, "I do belong here. I'm carrying on the legacy of our grandfather, Steven, who dreamed of unifying our kind with the other creatures in the land."

Spencer's eyes softened at the mention of his beloved father's name. He looked out to the horizon for a while before speaking. "I remember when my father used to take me, as a little porcupette, to play with the other animals. I even became playmates with a fox pup named Kenji. We used to roam the forest together every day." Mattie saw a look of deep fondness she had never seen in her father before. *This must be the young porcupine that Mom spoke of falling in love with.*

But then Spencer grimaced darkly and growled, "But no, they're all enemies and my father was too naive to see that! That's why a coyote killed him; he was a fool to believe in the goodness of other creatures!"

Mattie held her tongue, realizing that her father was working furiously to crush the openheartedness of his father that she refused to repress in her own veins. She so desperately wanted to tell them that even though a coyote had killed their grandfather, another coyote had saved her, as well as the entire clan, from imminent danger. There are both good and bad animals out there, but most of them wanted to help from her experience. She also didn't want to endanger Pearson, so she kept quiet.

Spencer motioned for everyone to calm down. "OK, let's settle down. Mattie's visiting so let's treat her like the honored guest she is."

Mattie shook her head. "When did your own flesh and blood become just a guest to you?"

Spencer paused for a moment and snapped, "When you broke from the responsibility and tradition of protecting the clan, to become a vagabond."

"I *am* carrying on the true tradition of the commander, which is about unity. Plus, you wanted to get rid of me the moment I was born because you were ashamed of me. All I wanted was your approval and attention and to bring honor to your name. But now I know for a fact that no matter what I achieve or accomplish, it will never be enough compared to having silly quills that took nothing to earn."

Mattie turned away from her father toward Josephine and Jasmine and murmured softly, pointing to where Pearson was hiding, "I'll be up by that juniper tree tonight, but I'll be leaving in the morning. Come by if you'd like to say goodbye."

Both Josephine and Jasmine nodded with tears in their eyes. Mattie turned her back toward her family and began her uphill trek back to Pearson. Hot tears fell down her cheek, though her grief was more for Josephine, Jasmine, Darius, and Katie because they would always be overlooked by the insular, insecure, alpha male-dominated clan that could never acknowledge the greatness of their power.

35

INTERWOVEN

During her hike, she saw a freshly woven web and went to check it out, hoping to find Mikey. When she examined it, it spelled, "I told you so."

She heartily laughed and shouted, "Mikey!"

He crawled out of the crevice of a tree and smirked. "Yeah, and I'm going to keep rubbing it in."

She leaped over and gazed into his eyes, grinning from ear to ear. "I missed you *so* much! I was afraid I'd never see you again. How did you know I was here?"

"Contrary to popular belief, once you care deeply for someone, it doesn't magically disappear. Trust me, I've tried. I've been watching your family for a while, hoping you'd return," Mikey replied.

Tears welled up in Mattie's eyes when she realized Mikey had never stopped being her loyal friend.

He climbed next to her. "I'm sorry I took off that night. I was just so hurt you couldn't see how committed I was to you just because I wasn't a porcupine."

"You don't need to apologize. I was so dense and blinded by my obsession for their approval," Mattie said.

Mikey beamed. "Well, I missed you and our trap-setting

days. I've been so bored; I just keep weaving webs over your family den to get back at Jasmine and Trevor since they're usually the first ones to come out in the evening."

Mattie chuckled, imagining her siblings repeatedly swatting away the webs with no clue as to why it kept happening. "I never told you, but I came alive helping you—it gave me a sense of purpose. I wasn't being overlooked for once. Most animals ignore me and don't give me the time of day," the spider lamented.

"Well, their loss because you're absolutely amazing. You taught me some of the most important lessons in life," Mattie said.

"What's that?"

Mattie smiled and said, "That I have so much to learn from other creatures. And that I have nothing to prove. The ones that matter already approve of me before I do anything, just like you did. You didn't care if I was a fat, skinny, popular, or shunned spineless porcupine. You were my friend through all of it."

"By the way, I always thought it wasn't a good idea that you were dieting," Mikey said.

Mattie chuckled. "Well, you were right. All those things I did for approval were a waste of time. I'm done with that. I'm fine just as I am."

"Are you sure? Seemed like you still wanted your family to approve of you based on your conversation with them," Mikey said.

Mattie chuckled. "Always the truth-teller just like I remember."

"Can't help it, I care about you," Mikey said and beamed.

Mattie thought about it and said, "Yeah, old habits are hard to break. But it's time to form a new clan, one of creatures of all shapes and sizes. One where we are seen for our hearts, and we know that our unique differences are our strengths. Wanna join us?"

Mikey said, "How are you going to find them?"

"Just like I found you, roaming the wilderness," Mattie said.

"Touché. Though I'm getting old. Lemme sleep on it." Mikey responded as he yawned.

Mattie nodded and stuck out her paw toward him. He tapped it just like he used to when they celebrated their traps together. Before he scurried back into a tree crevice, she said, "Love you, my friend."

Mikey blushed but spoke up, saying, "Yeah. Me, too."

36

TOO SMALL A CLAN

WHEN MATTIE APPROACHED PEARSON, HE ASKED, "So can I eat your dad and brother?"

Mattie laughed. "You saw all of that?"

"Of course, I was mesmerized—that was more death-defying than all the tricks you've ever performed," Pearson said, joking. He put his paw on her shoulder. "And way braver."

Mattie hugged Pearson. "It's probably the last time I'll see my dad. I needed to let him know how I felt."

"And you did. But the reality is, they're just too small a clan for you to lead," Pearson said.

"What do you mean?" Mattie asked.

"It's like what you said earlier to Christian. The circus was too small of a world for you. That's why it eventually spit you out."

Mattie looked confused.

He continued, "C'mon, would you truly be happy being born a porcupine with quills, living a small life within your clan? Sure, maybe you'd become commander, have a partner, kids, settle down. Then what? Wouldn't you rather live the adventure you've been on—being a star performer in a circus, becoming friends with a monkey, elephant, tree, owls, otters, bats, and exploring the wild with your favorite canine, an albino coyote?"

He snuggled up next to Mattie and, putting his paw to his ear, said, "What'd you say? Did I hear that right? Yeah, you did. A porcupine that's best friends with a coyote. I guarantee that'll be in the history books."

Mattie chuckled. "Yeah, I think that's a first."

"Exactly!" Pearson exclaimed.

Mattie walked around in circles musing, "Not to sound greedy, but why does it have to be either-or? I want both my clan and the wilderness."

Pearson nodded his head and sat for a moment in deep thought, then said, "What you want is completely valid and honestly, I want it, too. Remember how I was eventually captured by the circus because Hannah didn't want to be with me anymore? All I ever dreamed of, since I was a pup, was to start my own family. I wanted to be just like my dad —he was such a warmhearted, brave father. He loved all of us more than his own life. He's the one who modeled to me that we should not use others as a means to an end, but we should love others as the means and the end. And that's all I wanted to do for my little ones. But Hannah couldn't get past my exterior. It didn't help that her friends whispered whenever I came over, 'the albino is coming,' and quickly scattered. It hurt so much. Unfulfilled dreams are real and awful."

Pearson's head sank into his chest. Mattie came over and gave him a big embrace.

He snuggled back and said, "It'll never get old that a porcupine can hug me."

Mattie smiled, then consoled him by saying, "I'm sorry it's been so hard for you."

"For us," he said. "I sometimes wonder what it would've been like to have been born like every other coyote. I would've remained in my little band for the rest of my life roaming the land, hunting and killing animals instead of getting to know them for the treasure that they are. Like you," said Pearson.

Mattie blushed.

"You, the otters, the bats, and the trees have been better to me than most of my own band. The blood that runs through our veins doesn't make us family—it's the rhythm of our hearts beating in sync with one another. You know it in your bones when you connect. You realize you are on the same frequency, reading the same song sheet. It's like being in harmony with a tuning fork and your heart burns within you," Pearson said.

He shook his head, "Wow, I would've missed out on so much had I eaten you versus becoming your friend."

Mattie pulled back and gave him a weary look.

He put his paw on hers, "Hear me out. Sure, I could've nourished my body for one meal, but instead, I have hundreds of moments full of laughter, snuggles, and wisdom. I'm nourishing my soul through friendship. That's why I eat mostly berries, insects, fish, and occasionally annoying rats."

Mattie's eyebrows curled as she looked at Pearson, "Did you eat Roger?"

"No, but I really wanted to," Pearson admitted with embarrassment.

Mattie laughed. "I don't blame you. If I ate rats, I would've eaten him."

"The self-control it took, let me tell you," Pearson said.

Mattie smiled. "I'm proud of you, Pearson. I'm honored to be your friend. We are definitely in tune with each other."

"Right back at ya, commander," Pearson said with a bow.

They sat and watched Mattie's family head back into their dens to retire. Mattie's heart stirred with affection as she saw Jasmine playfully rounding up her adventurous porcupettes, who still wanted to explore the woods instead of turning in.

Mattie sighed, "I still want both."

"Me, too," Pearson said. "And that's fair, and it could still happen for us. We don't know the future. But maybe the reason we were born differently on the outside is because that matches our souls, which were always meant for bigger worlds. That's why nature decided to specifically mark us as unique, to make sure we wouldn't stay small. And we haven't. How many porcupines do you know that have gone on adventures like you, performed tricks on an elephant, spoken with a tree, and befriended so many different kinds of animals?"

"None," Mattie conceded.

"And it still doesn't take away from the loss of an ordinary life. We need to grieve that. But if you could only choose one kind of life, what would you choose? One with quills living like every other porcupine or one that's trailblazing a new path in the vast wilderness? You change the world simply by existing, Mattie."

"No, I refuse to be denied because of something outside my control! I still want both and I will do everything possible to bend reality toward my dreams. I've gone through so much heartache being who I am," Mattie snapped back. "When will the losses finally end? When will the upswing begin?"

"OK, then it's settled. Let's start a family," Pearson said as he stood up.

Mattie's eyes widened.

Pearson laughed. "No, not like that, we're different species. I mean, there's gotta be others out there who have been ostracized and orphaned like us—they need a family. Let's go find them and help them know they belong, like how we helped Christian."

Mattie nodded, her heart welling with compassion at the thought of providing much needed belonging to others like her.

"We'll have our families. Sure, they might not look like what we've imagined. But how much of our lives ever plays out like we imagined?" Pearson said.

Mattie thought back to the river and imagined herself surrendering to the current welling in her heart. "Yes, let's go find our family of misfits, rejects, and the hurting ones."

She felt such resolve and excitement for the adventure that lay before them. Instead of having a small porcupine clan to nurture and protect, she could potentially have dozens of different creatures all over the wilderness to care for and who desperately needed it, just like her. She felt love oozing out of every pore of her being. Looking up at the stars, she expressed her gratitude for being born without spines. At that moment, she realized that she was born perfectly designed on the outside to match the interior of her heart. Mattie wanted nothing other than to embrace others and give them a sense of family. Not having quills wasn't a weakness but a superpower. It was all a matter of context. She hugged herself, overwhelmed with gratitude for her soft, sensitive nature. Mattie couldn't wait to tell Jack and Michelle, who might also want to be a part of their family and explore the land to find others like them.

Indeed, everything happens for a reason, she thought. Under a tree, she cuddled up with Pearson against the cold night. Still, she felt a lingering tinge of sadness that she couldn't fully belong in her clan and start a little family with her own flesh and blood.

37

KIND TO OUR OWN KIND

Mattie awoke to hear Pearson growling at Jasmine, who was about to attack him with her quills.

"No, he's my friend!" Mattie yelled.

Jasmine backed down and Pearson shook off the adrenaline that was building in his veins.

"Wow, what a way to wake up," Mattie muttered in frustration.

Jasmine said, "You told Mom and me that we could come to say goodbye."

Mattie looked over at Pearson. "Oops, forgot to mention that. I was too engrossed in our conversation last night."

She looked at Jasmine and pointed at her favorite albino creature, "This is my best friend, Pearson."

Jasmine nodded. Mattie turned to Pearson, "And this is my sister, Jasmine."

"Howdy," Pearson said with a disarming grin.

Jasmine smirked and said, "I can see why he's your best friend."

"Yeah, he's a keeper," Mattie said as Pearson blushed.

Jasmine looked at Pearson. "As much as I like small talk,

Mom will be here soon, and I wanted to talk to you alone about something."

Mattie chuckled as she thought, *Jasmine's still the snippy porcupine full of attitude that I remembered. Some things never change.*

Pearson glanced over at Mattie, who nodded to let him know that she was OK. Before he left, he whispered to Mattie, "I'll be close if you need me."

Mattie nodded her thanks. As soon as Pearson was out of sight, Jasmine confessed, "I'm the one who sabotaged your traps. It's been eating at me all these years. I'm so sorry."

"I know," Mattie replied sadly, thinking of all the animals that were unintentionally killed.

"Dad made me do it. He told me it would be best for the clan because the traps would eventually fail and harm us. I was too young to know any better. Please forgive me," Jasmine said with tears in her eyes.

She continued, "And honestly, back then, I wanted you out of the picture because I was so jealous of you."

Mattie gasped in disbelief, "Jealous of *me*? Why?"

"Are you kidding, Mattie? I've always wondered what it'd be like to be spineless! And after hearing about all your adventures, now I really wish I was. It doesn't help that Katie and Darius can't stop raving about how cool you are and how they wish they were your spineless kids."

Mattie was in shock. She never would've imagined any porcupine wanting to trade places with her, let alone her sister.

"I always envied you. That's why I bullied you. You had Mom's full attention. And now I find out you were a circus star and you've explored the wilderness befriending other animals. What the heck?" Jasmine looked frustrated.

Mattie said, "Jasmine, it's not all that it's cracked up to be."

"Oh, really? Then tell me, what's it like to feel the wind,

the rain, the sun? Or what it's like to ride an elephant? What does their tusk feel like? How about the warmth of an otter and the cuddle of a bat? Tell me because I have no idea, nor ever will." Jasmine grumbled as tears trickled down her face.

"I've always wanted to feel. But no, I have spines just like every other porcupine. Hope you appreciate the precious gift you've been given!"

The tears turned into bitter sobbing. Mattie was blind-sided by Jasmine's anguish. This whole time, she had thought of herself as the unfortunate one and had wanted to be like Jasmine, a porcupine with quills. The story she had believed her entire life was that she was the cursed one, and her siblings were the blessed ones.

It was true though that she had gotten the better parent out of the deal. Jasmine and Trevor grew up with an abusive, manipulative tyrant while she had her mom's loving care all to herself.

Jasmine blurted out through her sobs, "I can't feel any of these things or ever will, Mattie. But you can. So, do it for me. Do it for all of us."

Mattie wanted so badly to give Jasmine the ability to feel. That's when a light bulb went off. She said, "Remember when you covered me in your quills?"

"This isn't the time to remind me of what a jerk I was," Jasmine said.

Mattie shook her head with excitement, "No, that's not what I meant. After that happened, Mom wanted to comfort me so badly that she placed all her quills in a tree. You can do that, too!"

"You can't be serious, Mattie."

Mattie said, "You want to know what it's like to be me, right?"

Jasmine nodded.

"So, disarm yourself. Sure, the clan will make fun of you and you'll be vulnerable until your quills grow back. But if you wanna know what it's like to feel, now's your chance," Mattie said enthusiastically. "I'll even have Pearson come over so you can feel what fur is like. You in?"

Jasmine's eyebrows curled. "I can't believe you really want me to do this."

"Better for you to feel the rain, wind, and sun than me describing it to you," Mattie said.

"Is it worth it?" Jasmine asked.

Mattie said, "Well, the only time I had quills was when you put them in me and that was definitely worse than being naked."

Jasmine said, "If anything, I should do this as payback for being so atrocious to you."

"There's no should or shouldn't. If you do things out of obligation instead of desire, they will ultimately backfire. Do it only if *you* want to, OK?" Mattie said.

Jasmine stared at the juniper tree where Mattie had been sleeping under just moments earlier. Her eyes filled with resolve. She went over and pressed all of her quills into the tree.

Mattie brimmed with joy that she could finally share her unique gift with her sister.

The sun began to rise, and its rays bathed Jasmine's newly naked skin. Jasmine danced as its warmth covered her.

Mattie smiled. "So, how does it feel?"

"Heavenly," Jasmine said, grinning broadly.

Mattie shouted for Pearson to come over and he appeared, amazed at the sight of Jasmine spineless.

"Wanna know what it's like to be cradled by a furry friend?" Mattie asked Jasmine.

Jasmine hesitated and asked, "Are you sure he's safe?"

"Safer than most porcupines I know," Mattie said.

Jasmine smiled. "Ain't that the truth."

Mattie motioned Pearson over. "She wants to know what fur feels like."

Pearson smiled and pranced over to Jasmine, who still looked apprehensive. The warmhearted albino creature reached out his paw slowly and motioned for her to feel his fur. Jasmine gradually reached out, and as she felt Pearson's fur, her eyes lit up.

"That feels so funny," Jasmine said.

Pearson joked, "Hey, who are you calling funny?"

"That's not what I meant," Jasmine said.

Pearson chuckled. "I know, I'm just teasing."

Jasmine relaxed. Pearson truly had a gift of winning others over with his gentle humor. After a while of Jasmine rubbing his paw, he asked, "Can I give you a hug?"

Jasmine grinned, but her defensive, porcupine nature got the best of her and she shook her head. Pearson nodded but looked disappointed by her response to his vulnerability.

Nearby, leaves rustled and Pearson resumed a defensive posture. Then Josephine appeared through a bush.

"Mom!" Mattie yelled with delight.

Josephine grinned, "I'll never get tired of hearing you say that."

Mattie went over and Josephine put her paw gently on Mattie's. Then Josephine looked over at Jasmine and smirked. "Great, I have two naked daughters. What will the clan say now?" Josephine said with a giggle.

Then she walked over to another tree. "Well, they'll need to talk about their naked mama, too," and she also put her quills into a tree.

Jasmine shouted, "Mom, you'll be defenseless!"

"It's OK, my time is near and there's nothing I want more than to feel the touch of both my daughters before I go," Josephine said.

Mother motioned for her daughters to come close and she embraced them. Pearson got misty-eyed observing their profound moment of reconciliation.

Josephine asked Pearson, "Are you the one who kept my baby safe?"

He nodded, "She wasn't too bad at protecting herself though."

"Don't I know it. She's a fighter, isn't she?" Josephine said.

She kissed both Mattie and Jasmine on their foreheads as she said, "Both of my babies are, with or without quills."

She looked into Mattie's eyes, then whispered to her, "You're more than I could've ever hoped for. You've lived up to your name, 'Strength in Battle, Strong in War,' and then some. And to me, you will always be a commander."

Mattie's eyes welled up with tears and her heart swelled with pride. Josephine said with authority, "Just because you can't be the commander of this little clan doesn't mean you can't be a leader out in the vast wilderness. I always knew your heart was too big to be contained in this valley. You were made to represent the best of our kind to every other kind."

"Come with me," Mattie insisted to both her mom and sister. She pointed to Pearson. "Now that you're both spineless, you can ride on top of him."

Pearson smiled, saying, "I've gotten pretty good at balancing naked porcupines on my back."

Josephine chuckled, then cradled Mattie's face with her paw, "Then what happens when our spines grow back?"

"Keep putting them into trees," Mattie answered excitedly.

Jasmine was tempted by the idea but said, "I can't leave my family."

Josephine hugged Mattie, "You were made for this, not us."

Mattie felt the weight of her mom's words like a divine mandate.

Jasmine embraced Mattie. "Please do it for me, for Mom, for all of us who can't. We'll be with you in spirit."

Mattie sighed. She knew it was true; it wasn't meant for anyone but her. She had the heart, the compassion, and the hard-earned wisdom from her journey that no one else had. All of this had accumulated to make her perfect at building bridges with other creatures.

The naked porcupines all shared one long, final embrace. Jasmine motioned over to Pearson. "Is it too late to change my mind about that hug?"

Pearson shook his head and went over to join the big cuddle fest. Jasmine especially loved the feeling of being cradled by a furry creature.

After they had spent all morning snuggling, it was time for Jasmine and Josephine to return to their den. And for Mattie, it was time to return to her true home, the vast wilderness with all of its mysteries, creatures, and the misfit family she was yet to create—for her mom, for Jasmine, for Katie, for Darius, for her clan, and for porcupines everywhere who couldn't because they were unwilling to let their defenses down. Mattie would live up to her name and carry on the commander's legacy, unifying creatures against the wilderness' true evil—separation due to fear, misunderstanding, and past wounds. Darius and Katie gave her hope that the next generation could be different. But she knew she had to help pave the road for embracing other creatures so they could more easily follow her footsteps.

She took one more look at the valley of her agonized youth. It dawned on her that as far as the east was from the west, that was how immense the expanse was between her once insecure, self-loathing childhood and where she stood today. She absolutely cherished being the world's one and only truly spineless porcupine.

Still, she couldn't shake the haunting sadness of leaving her clan. She longed to return and show her homogenous clan the beauty of the wilderness and all the creatures that reside in it. If she couldn't convince them to leave, she planned to bring her adopted, heterogeneous family to her clan one day. She hoped it would be while her father was still alive, and she could unite both her adopted and blood family.

As Pearson and Mattie were about to take off, Mikey appeared and smiled. "Hey, you're not leaving without me."

He hopped over to his usual spot on Mattie, right above her ear, and the three of them headed through the valley. She introduced Mikey and Pearson. "Pearson, meet Mikey, my first friend. He taught me that the ones we overlook often have the greatest wisdom to offer."

Then she added, "Oh, and he also taught me how to build traps."

Pearson grinned broadly at Mikey and nodded in gratitude. Mattie then leaned her ear toward Pearson so Mikey could get a closer look at him. "And Mikey, this is Pearson. He taught me that we aren't made for the circus of efficiency, productivity, and control. But we *are* perfectly built for love and belonging."

Mikey jokingly said, "Is that it? Sorry, bud. She wouldn't have talked to you if it wasn't for me. I'm the winner this round."

Pearson belly laughed. "I can tell we're going to get along swimmingly."

Mikey winked at Pearson with a grin.

Mattie wondered how they would find the misfits, but then she remembered Christian and what Pearson had said about family. She picked up two sticks on the path that were roughly the same shape and size. Mattie then played her heart's rhythm onto the ground. It echoed throughout the valley and she knew it would resonate with the ones that were meant to join their fold. And it did. Animals began popping their heads out, curious about the unique, offbeat cadence. They were drawn to this new sound as if awakened by a yearning deep within them. Several crawled out of their caves and dens and ventured toward its source. They were all shapes and sizes, colors, and species. Though each one of them would have to defy their fears, self-doubt, and often-times, long-held traditions, to answer the wild pounding of their hearts—the pulse that beat within them for a brighter future where the wilderness could be a family where all belonged, were held and were safe.

THE END

ACKNOWLEDGMENTS

This book was seven years in the making and it would not have been finished in a timely manner and in its finest form without **Charlotte Ashlock**, my dear friend and phenomenal developmental editor. We met weekly for over a year to bring this story to life even when I wanted to give up. You carried me on your back on multiple occasions to get this across the finish line. I am so deeply grateful for you.

Everyone below has helped shape this book in a significant way. Thank you from the depths of my heart.

Pearson

When I was fifteen years old, You came into my Story and have never failed to show me that You are Love. You gave this spineless porcupine a place to belong, in Your arms. Let's keep welcoming all the misfits, troublemakers, and outcasts home to their own hearts.

Editors

To Amanda Chung, Amanda Harman, Gina Goldblatt, Jeanne Wong, Jill French, J. J. Chang, Katie Cheng, Madeline Miles, Rachel Loui, Antonio Ingram, Maddie Reardon,

Brittany Williams (BSPOKEiT), Lucy Tang, Eric Ho, Tina Razzell, and Illumify Media: I appreciate you taking the time to read through the manuscript and making key suggestions on how to take Mattie's story to the next level. I also wanted to give a special shout-out to Grammarly for being a wonderful digital writing assistant.

Illustrator

Karl Ni, from the moment I saw your sketch of Mattie, I knew you understood the heart of this book. Thank you for visualizing Mattie and Pearson to the world.

Endorsers

William Paul Young, Carin Taylor, Ken Fong, Pádraig Ó Tuama, and Vivian Wong: thank you for lending your credibility to this labor of love. But more importantly, thanks for being mentors and friends through thick and thin. I love you.

Friends

Charlotte Ashlock, Michelle Qi, Jeanne Wong, Cynthia Yu, Shaowei Lin, Joanne Lee, Gina Goldblatt, Karena & Todd Lout, Darius Brown, Helen G. Caddie-Larcenia, Joyce Wang, Rhi Alexander, Stephanie Frigault, Melanie DeSessa, Jaime Ng, Andrew Abad, Colin McAvoy, Mike Luong, Madeline Miles, Tony Le, Cassie Brazil, Rachel Loui, Rene Chu, Vanness Wu, Olivia Price, Pacia Dewald, Tejasvi Jaladi, Debbie Ulanday, Tom Emanuel, Jacqueline Klotz, Diane & Clayton Jung, Roger Hsu, Roxanne Sweatt, Timothy Hornstine, Amanda Harman, Thuy Vy Bui, Theresa Christian, Chiang Wan-an & Jane Shih, Dr. Michael Sanchez, Chris and Alie Scott, Johanna Torres, Dev Cuny, Leslie Rayno, Greg & Andi Steward, and the Oak Life Church community & LGBTQ+ small group, Lyrical Opposition crew, and Workday PRIDE & The Talented Tenth EBCs: you strengthened and supported me when I thought I could no longer stand in the truth of who I am. Thank you for giving me the courage to press on and arise unashamed and loved.

Family

My parents, especially my dad, encouraged me to write this book and pursue my creative endeavors. Thank you, Mom, Dad, Gloria, and Jenny, for your faithful love and support. Special shout-out to the Chungs, Yangs, Chengs, Kaus, and Chens for meeting weekly through shelter-in-place, supporting me through the final stages of this project, and giving me a sense of community.

My Late Uncle Shing Peter Kau

If it weren't for you introducing my parents and playing matchmaker, my sisters and I would not be here today. Thank you for patiently teaching me how to ski and always going out of your way to connect and hear about our lives. I loved seeing how much you cherished life and your beloved wife, Nancy, your son, Albert, and his wife, Melissa, as well as your grandchildren. I'm especially grateful for you and Nancy's generous support of my book in the twilight of your life. We miss and love you, dearly. I hope this book is an honorable tribute to your legacy.

For more on SAY and *The Spineless Porcupine*, please visit:
www.SAYYang.com

CPSIA information can be obtained
at www.ICGtesting.com
Printed in the USA
FSHW011952050321
79243FS